THE LAST LETTER

LARRY REYNOLDS

iUniverse

THE LAST LETTER

Copyright © 2023 Larry Reynolds.

All rights reserved. No part of this book may be used or reproduced by any means, graphic, electronic, or mechanical, including photocopying, recording, taping or by any information storage retrieval system without the written permission of the author except in the case of brief quotations embodied in critical articles and reviews.

iUniverse books may be ordered through booksellers or by contacting:

iUniverse
1663 Liberty Drive
Bloomington, IN 47403
www.iuniverse.com
844-349-9409

Because of the dynamic nature of the Internet, any web addresses or links contained in this book may have changed since publication and may no longer be valid. The views expressed in this work are solely those of the author and do not necessarily reflect the views of the publisher, and the publisher hereby disclaims any responsibility for them.

Any people depicted in stock imagery provided by Getty Images are models, and such images are being used for illustrative purposes only. Certain stock imagery © Getty Images.

ISBN: 978-1-6632-5453-5 (sc)
ISBN: 978-1-6632-5454-2 (e)

Library of Congress Control Number: 2023912927

Print information available on the last page.

iUniverse rev. date: 09/07/2023

Clasped tightly in my hand was a letter that revealed the sealed fate of an old friend. The details of that fate were as unclear to me at that moment as the journey I would be willed to take in order to discover them.

It was all so absurd. So unusual. A karmic practical joke with no punch line.

It was my choice to walk through the double-glass doors to the post office counter to step into my friend's menagerie of demise. I have both embraced and regretted that choice ever since.

THE LAST LETTER
Winter, 1998

CHAPTER 1

THE VERY EXTRAORDINARY ORDINARY DAY

It was an early October day. A Thursday, I think. Like every weekday, I pulled onto Monroe Street in Pleasantville, the small Iowa town where I have spent all of my life, except for four years of college an hour away from home pursuing a degree in literature.

With a degree in hand and no opportunities to present it to, I have worked as an occupational therapist at the

Veterans Administration Hospital in Knoxville, a fifteen-minute drive from home, for eleven years. It is and has been, a comfortable job with modest rewards and far fewer risks than trying to support a family as a writer. The comfort is derived primarily from predictability versus any general sense of satisfaction.

My workday ends at 3:00 p.m. I pull into downtown--a single road with two blocks of buildings in different stages of decay, a bank, and a post office. By 3:45 p.m. I am usually sitting on one of six single, worn stools at the Rose City Café to have a slice of one of three different types of pie—apple, pecan, and cherry--and a cup of coffee. The café owner, cook, and waitress, Shelly Benson, has been a friend since grade school, taking over the café from her parents and, very likely, their parents before them. She is a welcome and friendly face in the transition from my work day to my duties as a father and husband each evening.

The café, I assume, is not dissimilar to thousands of small-town cafes across the country on any given day in any given season. There are typically five or six locals in the afternoon, nearly always middle-aged and older men, and while the roster changes from time to time the content of conversation is always the same. The range of topics includes grain prices and crop conditions, weather, various aches and pains—some new, some more imaginary--and an occasional bit of scandalous and unproven gossip about any individual but the ones in the immediate proximity.

The conversation always—ALWAYS—migrates to the sports history and legends of the local high school, as well as the emerging stars that all seem to be "going places" but seldom ever do. This is the full range of topics, presented in no particular order, and with minimal variation. I have long been convinced that aliens could invade my small town and unless they scored three touchdowns in 1982 against Melcher-Dallas, the local rival, there would be no talk of it at the cafe.

For any "foreigner"—anyone that has not lived in a small town in the Midwest—there is a special nuance to the fall that cannot be found anywhere else on earth. The autumn sun's slow daily crawl to the west provides a color spectrum and clarity that the most sophisticated camera lens cannot adequately capture. The air is crisp and mildly sweet with the smell of drying crops—corn and soybeans—that cover the landscape like a warm quilt pattern stitched by God himself. Thousands of dry, fallen leaves make their slow, poetic dance to nowhere in the mild breeze, creating a symphony of light harmonic scratches along the blacktop roads and jigsaw cracks of old sidewalks. It is all so subtle. So beautiful. And, I have not taken it for granted as long as I have lived.

I finished my pie—pecan on this particular day--and coffee, trying to decide the carry-home value of any of the café banter that I could share with my wife of thirteen years, Debbie. There usually isn't, and I'm left to comment on the flavor and freshness of my pie and coffee. Flavors and recipes that haven't changed in decades, but still provide a conversation starter for an evening at home.

It is a placid life. Comforting. Common. Predictable. This Thursday was like so many before it and, in my mind, so many to come.

The last stop on my weekday ritual is the post office to pick up our mail. In rural areas, you can opt for the slower rural mail delivery, or you can save a few days on bills, magazines, and letters by paying for a post office box at the local post office. Those couple of days are like the difference between FedEx overnight and pony express, so it is well worth the forty-seven dollars a year to "lease" the post office box.

There are singular, sudden events that change the course of a person's life. They are rare and never arrive with nuance. The sudden death of a friend or family member. An accident. A winning lottery ticket. Finding that first-glance lover, or losing them just as quickly. There are also those events that change the course of life, but offer the luxury of time to prepare—to consider the many paths available and move forward with confidence and vision. The coming birth of a child. The long, slow death of a loved one. A career opportunity. Declining health. A college degree. I never thought about the difference, never HAD to think about the difference, until this very different Thursday in October. This day the third—and most challenging—type of event was merely a short walk across the street at the United States Post Office in Pleasantville, Iowa, 50225.

The third and most challenging sudden event, of course, is one that will change the course of life with no nuance, no luxury to prepare, and come with so many possible paths that you are left frozen in that moment, paralyzed on how to proceed and realizing quickly that you will never again be able to return to the moments before it.

A small-town post office is an amazing work of design simplicity, function, and consistency. There are two mailboxes outside the entrance—one for "local" letters and the other for "out of town" mail. The United States flag

THE LAST LETTER

wisps in the wind with the flag chain tapping against the metal pole like a subtle bell tower with no particular cadence and a welcoming tone.

Through the glass double doors there is a wall of three hundred post office boxes of various sizes, which seems optimistic for a town our size with a population that hasn't changed since the turn of the century. Each post office box has a small, sturdy pure brass door with a three-letter combination lock that, I assume, would be very simple to "crack" if one were so inclined. There is a small glass window at the top of each so you can see if there is enough mail to make the effort worth your while.

To the right of the P.O. Box-wall is the FBI's Most Wanted posters, each face as nefarious as the next, and postal bulletins that have been posted on the aluminum-framed corkboard since the beginning of time. There is also a counter with a pen on a chain for any last-minute duties, a waste can, and another American flag next to the Iowa state flag.

To the left of the wall is another set of glass double doors that leads to "the counter". The counter is the realm of the Postmaster, or in the case of Pleasantville since--I believe--the Pony Express, the Postmistress. This is where the business of the post office takes place and where you access the collective postal wisdom of Jeanne Schumann, who may possibly be the oldest postal employee on the planet.

Jeanne may be sixty, or one hundred and four, because her appearance—from dress to hair, shoes to nails--has not changed since I would go in with my mother to buy stamps as a child. My father used to joke that she was a waitress before she began her postal employ and when anyone would ask where, he would respond, "The Last Supper."

Jeanne has always been kind, yet straightforward, and will openly quote every postal regulation, process, and rule word-for-word. As such, she is all business, all the time. She does have an affinity for children and still keeps a large box of Tootsie Pops for any child up to the age of ten. I know this very specific milestone because when I was around ten my mom sent me to the counter to buy stamps for her while she was across the street at Doc Powell's veterinary clinic with our family dog. After I procured the stamps and asked for a Tootsie Pop, Jeanne dropped her head so her dark gray eyes could clear the boundaries of her reading glasses and curtly appointed, "You're big enough to walk down to Gilderbroom's Grocery and buy your own."

Charity, it turns out, has a shelf life and in Jeanne's case, it is just before adolescence.

Make no mistake, Jeanne's stoic demeanor has no relationship to her intimate knowledge of each of the 1,500 denizens of our small Iowa town. Most people live under the illusion that the epicenter for information big and small in a town is the café or the hair salon. Generally, the café for the men—although Frank's barber shop in the basement of the State Bank is a close second; and, the salon for women and those unfortunate children that have to accompany them for their weekly "touch up".

While there is a topical type of truth to all of that, all information flows through the post office and, therefore, through Jeanne Schumann. She looks at every envelope that is sent out of town, within town, and knows who is sending what to whom and how often. Bills. Checks. Love letters.

THE LAST LETTER

Magazines. Letters to and from faraway places. Birthday and Christmas cards and presents. Nothing escapes the watchful purview of the Moses of the Mailbox.

Occasionally, she will tip her hand. I have picked up parcels from my sister in Omaha to my family—usually, birthday presents for the kids. Jeanne will always make it a point to say, "Aunt Karen sure does love your boy. And she always gets his present here a week before his birthday."

It usually isn't until ten minutes after I leave the post office that I realize she recalls the day my son was born and without opening a single letter or package has a very good sense of the contents within. It is an impressive almanac she maintains, and she maintains it every day except federal holidays and the three weeks the postal service provides for vacation based on her years of dutiful service.

I walked through the main doors of the post office and walked to Post Office Box 615. With three quick right turns to clear the combination, I stopped at "A", then to the left one full rotation past "G", and back to the right for "F". After the telltale "click", I slid the lever to open the small brass door. I pulled out a Popular Mechanics magazine and two bills, along with possibly the most tattered, light blue envelope I had ever seen. My name and address were faded but legible, though in handwriting that seemed familiar, yet not enough to place. Beyond the "USA" flag stamp and the address were creases, streaks, and stains that gave the appearance of a long, difficult journey to its final destination between the thumb and forefinger of my left hand. I tapped it against the magazine looking for clues and the only revelation came from the postmark, "Navajo Nation-Kayenta, Arizona". It was post-marked six days prior.

I usually thumb through the mail, walk back to the car, and sort through the this and thats of the day when I get home. That Thursday in October, curiosity would not allow it. I went to the small counter in the post office box area, set my other mail down, and opened the letter. Many days have passed in which I wish I had not, and a few that I give thanks I did.

CHAPTER 2

THE LAST LETTER

I am a methodical sort. I open most letters with the quick, crisp tear of a stainless steel letter opener at home that I recall we received as a gift from a relative, but the insignificance of the gesture never allowed us to remember when, who, or why. Today, I used the seemingly brutish alternative of prying my right index finger under the fold and tearing my way across the mystery that lied within. I pulled out a folded, four-page, single-spaced handwritten letter that to this day I can recite and recall every word, period, and punctuation. It said:

"Larry, by the time you read this, I will be very pleased and very dead. I will be happy because in this shit pile I find myself in, I had a plan, and—if you receive this—my plan actually worked. The thought of anything going as planned at this moment seems like a one-in-a-fucking-million odd. The notion you might get this is one of the few things I can hold hope for in my current situation. It's that very situation that confirms I'm dead. Dead as hell. Way fucking dead. I just don't know how long I've been dead, where I've died, or the points and people between here and where you are now that serve as my purpose—and now your purpose—for this letter."

I paused. Jesus. My brow shifted into a puzzled gaze and back to the pages with an intensity of focus that I recall perfectly, but will never be able to explain. I read on.

"About a week ago, after a couple of months, several doctor visits, and a ton of bullshit tests and speculation, I found myself sitting in the exam room of Dr. Steven Glasgow, an oncologist at Chicago Rush Hospital. Good guy. Long story short, Dr. Steve explained I have a tumor in my stomach—"metastasized gastric melanoma, stage III." The stink of the deal is the melanoma. It's fucking skin cancer that somehow brewed up and into a few

THE LAST LETTER

of the layers of my stomach. Skin cancer grows fast as hell, and the stage three part means it has or is definitely going to, spread to fuck knows where.

Dr. Steve gave me options that reminded me of Jon Booker's eternal question in high school: If you were neck-deep in snot and someone threw a bucket of shit at you, would you duck your head or sit and take it?

Option A was surgery to take out as much of my stomach as needed—likely most of it—as well as any lymph nodes around it that looked suspect. Then an aggressive course of chemotherapy and all the fun that comes with it, along with several big, bad doses of radiation. 6 to 12 months of bullshit that Dr. Steve said would give me a couple of years if it all went well. I asked if it ever all goes well.

He said, "Usually not. This isn't the kind of cancer you cure."

Fuck that. I asked him if I could at least get a handjob out of the deal and he didn't flinch. Not even a good-guy smirk. No high-fives. I guess it's his job to tell you you're fucked as straight up as can be, and I guess my job is to respect that.

I asked him what options B, C, and D were and he said they weren't. Option A is all I got. Seriously, fuck that!

"What if I don't do it?"

He went through the timeline and symptoms I'd experience and figured I'd be dead in around six months. I might get a couple more months than that if I was lucky. Lucky? Yeah, I was feeling real fuckin 'lucky' about then. Maybe less than six. He said it's hard to say. I told him I had to think about it and would let him know in a few days.

Three hours later, I called him. I thanked him. I told him I'm going with my own option. This option. The "fuck you" option. He asked if I wanted a second opinion, but I didn't need it. I had my second opinion and I was the one that made it. In those 3 hours, I thought of watching my grandma Bea fight cancer for four years and how fucked it was for her, for me, and for our family. No thanks. It was an easy decision. I wasn't going to die of cancer. I was going to live hard and die how and when the hell I wanted. You can let Blue Oyster Cult know that I don't fear the reaper, but I'm going to bend the reaper over and have my way with him!

For a few seconds, I thought about some cool suicide options, but I'm not a pussy, so that was off the table as soon as it got on it. I thought about catching a plane to Australia or the Himalayas to die somewhere I've never been. Dying on foreign soil seemed unpatriotic to me. Not that I'm a huge patriot, it just seemed pretty fucking empty and, with my current luck, the fucking plane would crash getting me there.

In the past week, I've made my peace for the most part and I've hatched my plan. This plan. I quit my job. Got out of my lease. Sold most of my shit. Bought some gear and planned to hit the road. I closed my bank account here in Chicago and sent a certified check to John Franey at the Pleasantville State Bank- -$92,869 (yes, advertising been bery, bery good to me)—and called him to tell him I wanted to open an account that I could draw from with a credit card or checks for as long as it would last. He shot me back some paperwork and told me my checks and card would be here in a few days. He agreed to pay the monthly card balance from my account so I had the statements sent directly to him. I'm good to go.

I also sent him an envelope with your name in it, told him to keep it until someone came in to ask for it, then open the envelope and if the name matched the person, give them what

THE LAST LETTER

is left—hopefully not a damn dime. Your next stop ought to be the bank. Franey will take it from there.

Took me a few days to figure out my wheels. The getaway car from the life that is being stolen from me. I was like fucking Goldilocks. The car option didn't last long. Dying in a car sounded skanky—that's what perverts do. I looked at a Harley. Rode it and figured I'd die of kidney failure before the cancer got me. Rough ride. Tried a Ducati. Badass bike. If James Bond had cancer, that's what he'd die on. I settled for a stripped-down Honda Goldwing Interstate 1500. Power, storage, smooth. Almost fuckable. It was a dick move, but I financed it. 25% down with the first payment in six months. They were optimists, not me.

I take off in about a week. I am inviting all my Chicago paesanos, as many women as possible, and maybe a few felons just to add some spice to a party this Friday. I plan to tell them I'm going to work overseas for a few years. Going away parties are always a cross between Christmas and the Fourth of July—the melancholy, memories, and warmth injected with high octane, three-stage fireworks. I'm going for insanity, but if debauchery is all I get, I'll still be happy. Besides, people don't need to know the details. They don't want the details. They want the party, and the party is what they'll get.

So here we are. You and me. I plan to write as I go and I need a co-pilot. I don't want the sadness shit so I'm not telling my family. They already think I'm going to Dubai—seemed like the most remote place they'd never want to visit—to work at an agency there. Guess it's up to you if, or how, they get closure. I don't have the stomach for it right now. Get it? Don't have the stomach for it. Fuck, I'm funny!

I couldn't trust something like this with anyone. I trust

you. Always have. And, you're the most talented writer I've ever met—and I work with writers!—so if someone can make some sense out of all this, it's you. Take a bow. Listen to the applause. You're a special mother fucker about now.

<u>THIS IS FUCKING IMPORTANT!</u>: I called Jeanne at the post office. I sent a check for a two-year lease on a PO Box. Box 269. Combination isn't important. I asked Jeanne to keep all the mail for that box behind the counter and I'd let her know who to give it to when the time came. She puked out some post office rules and I reminded her that she and my Grandma Bea were bridge clubbers and friends for too many years to count and I needed a favor. Took a little arm twistin' and the sacred memory of a pure soul, but even Jeanne can be charmed.

Take this letter to Jeanne and tell her you need the letters to PO Box 269. I hope it's more than just a few.

Give my love and regards to Debbie and the kids. They're very lucky, and so are you."

It was signed, *"This Is Fucked, Right????"* with a very large signature—*"T. Scott McGuire"*

I shook my head and laughed. Based on the author, I was certain this was a prank. I knew I would walk into Jeannie's counter, ask for the contents of the post office box, and there would be a single package with some symbolic, sophomoric artifact and a note that would say, "You're still SOOO fucking gullible!" Tracy was an ass like that--a "let's all laugh" ass. I did know it was authentic, not by the handwriting, but by the signature. When Tracy moved to Chicago after college, he starting using "T. Scott" or "Scott" because he thought his given name would not provide the appearance of intellect or relevance he needed to succeed.

THE LAST LETTER

I left the rest of my mail on the counter and walked through the double glass doors to Jeannie's counter with the letter still in my hand.

"Hey Jeannie, good afternoon."

She pushed her glasses up along the bridge of her nose, barely looking up.

"Larry," she acknowledged, her tone somewhat common and perfunctory.

I smiled and held up the letter in my left hand. "I need the contents of Post Office Box 269."

Jeannie froze. Everything common and perfunctory drained from her demeanor, including the last bit of skin tone from her stoic face. She literally went white.

"Box 269?" she repeated, although we both knew I was very clear on my initial question. She looked as though she had seen a ghost, a look in all the years that I have known her I have never seen.

Without unlocking her gaze, now riveted to mine, she slowly pulled off her reading glasses and let them hang from the bead chain around her neck.

"You're the one," she simply said.

"I guess," I responded. "I have a letter here that..."

Before I could finish my explanation, she turned around and marched her five-foot-six, semi-cylindrical body to a back area of the sorting room with a gate that can best be described as a city park teeter-totter with a broken hinge.

She returned dragging a large, thick burlap postal bag across the floor. It was around three-feet high and cinched tightly with a cord at the top. She hoisted it up to the counter. It seemed particularly heavy. There was no single letter that revealed the prank. There was no punchline. There was just me staring for what seemed like days at the bag and Jeanne staring at me. Not a single word was said. We were like two prospectors that found a cursed treasure of gold at the same time using different maps. There were only questions. There were no answers.

I finally broke the silence. "How long have the letters been coming in?"

"About every day for several months," she replied.

"That is a pretty big bag. How many letters does one of those things hold?"

"Letters?" Jeanne asked, answering herself just as quickly. "There are plenty of letters. There are also parcel post packages and a few small boxes."

"What am I supposed to do with these?" I asked, incredulously.

She shuffled quickly back into her Postmistress role. "Larry, these are your letters now. By law, they are no longer the property of the United States Postal Service."

I was looking for more holistic guidance, but that was the guidance I was given.

I nearly blurted out, "No. Really. What the hell am I supposed to do with these?!" Jeannie was as unsettled as I was, although much better at disguising it, so I did not want to escalate the already bizarre situation. Nor did I want her to ask the most crucial question: "What was in the letter? THAT letter." The letter still clasped in my lefthand.

I realized this was my issue, my burden. I would not be able to share it with anyone until I could better understand it myself. I had not yet decided if this was even a journey I was willing to take, but I knew whether I took the journey or not, it had to be without accomplices.

"Mind if I take the bag home and empty the contents? I can get the bag back to you in a few days if it is going to be an issue with the Post Office." I asked knowing the answer: the bag was postal property and could not be removed from the premises so I would have to return with my own bags. Yet, in that moment she looked at me knowing she was just as confused-- yet far less frantic.

She gave a warm and uncharacteristic response, "Yes, Larry. Just return the bag as soon as you can so no one gets in trouble." Even though we both knew no one would get in trouble.

It did not take "a little arm twistin'," or charm. It took a situation with a gravity all its own, and a gravity that had pulled her slowly, subtly, and strongly for several months. She knew it was time for her to release herself from that gravitational pull, that growing, impalpable wonder, and let me take her place in that orbit. It was now my riddle to solve and she was absolved of any further effort to understand it.

She had kept enough secrets for enough years about enough people that she had no interest in bearing this burden, and certainly no interest in bearing witness to it further. The transfer was complete as I clutched the bag and carried it out the doors, grabbed my other mail, and scurried quickly out of the main doors and to my car where I hurriedly placed it in my trunk.

I sat in my car for a few minutes trying to decide what to do. I could throw the bag in an alley dumpster and relieve myself of a duty I was called to do, but very unsure whether I could fulfill. I could drop the bag off at Tracy's aunt's house, as she was the only member of his family still in town. Not an option—I would have to find out where she lived, not difficult in a town of 1,500, but not an extra step I wanted to take at that moment. I could find out where his brother and sister lived now and find a way to get all of this to them. Or try to find his mom, wherever she may be. They had all left the area years ago.

The thought of dropping this on anyone's doorstep seemed as though I would be complicit in a crime I did not commit. It was too complicated. I needed simplicity. I felt like I had a nuclear bomb in my trunk and wherever I would take it there would be collateral damage. Yet, a friend—a friend I had not seen in a few years and knew most of my life—had trusted me with his dying wish.

It was a problem with no clear solution. I had been sitting in my car for several minutes on the main street of my small town, which would clearly be noticed by someone, somehow, at some point. I would have no explanation if they were to stop and ask, which is what residents of small towns do. In a small town, loitering begets inquisition and the answers to any questions are often carried well past the conversation at hand. I started my car and drove slowly out of town where the next best step became very clear.

I stopped at the Casey's convenience store on the north edge of town on my way home. Feeling as if I had a dead body in my backseat, I tried to calmly walk in. I went directly to the counter and asked Trinda for my demon of choice, a purchase I hadn't made in seven years: a pack of Camel cigarettes, non-filtered—Camel straights--and a book of matches.

She grabbed my drug of choice, smiled innocently, and said, "Does Debbie know about this?"

I just laughed uncomfortably, trying not to sweat, and

said, "I'm buying them for a friend, but it's best we just keep that to ourselves."

My "friend" was the writer I used to be. He always thought—and wrote—better with the incense-like slow burn of a Camel cigarette. I knew I would need his help to decide what to do, or whether to do anything at all. It was time to wake my old companion from a several-year slumber and the best way to do that was the strong, smooth waft of pure tobacco wrapped in thin paper.

Cigarettes and matches in the glove box. Imaginary dead body in the backseat. Nuclear bomb in the trunk. I was ready to go home. I pulled down our long, gravel drive two miles from town, grabbed the usual mail from the car, and walked into the house as if it was any other day. After dinner and tucking the kids in bed, I told Debbie I forgot to take a few things from work to my shop. In the cover of darkness, I took the bag out of the trunk and the cigarettes from the glove box, and then put them in my shop, a converted garage with enough clutter to let it lie until I decided what to do. I was out of the heat of the moment. I was relieved. And, I was exhausted.

CHAPTER 3

THE SLOW, SIMMERING BURN

A pack of Camel straight cigarettes contains twenty individual, tightly-wrapped cigarettes. Twenty opportunities for calm and clarity. I started my secret addiction in college. I was working on a short story for a creative writing class and could not get past the first sentence for hours.

I had formed my ideas, characters, theme, and plot quickly, but once I put my pencil in my hand and stared at the narrow-lined paper for my draft, everything disappeared and then came back in fragments and misalignment—brilliant thoughts with no glue to bind them nor the order necessary to frame a decent story correctly. Unlike painting, writing is an art that is guided by both abstract and order; inspiration and rules. Jackson Pollack could not write, and a good writer cannot write like Jackson Pollack paints.

I went out of the student union to try to clear my head and noticed Brad Morris, a senior literature major that had a far better sense of craft than me, as I was only a sophomore. He exuded the confidence that only wisdom, experience, and a wide field of view can provide.

He was sitting under a large oak tree just outside the union smoking a cigarette. I engaged in the usual small talk and mentioned I never knew he smoked.

"A good cancer stick or two helps me think, and definitely helps me write.", he announced in a matter-of-fact manner.

I admired Brad based on the few classes we had shared. He offered keen insights and deep passion in class, so this small revelation was like Hemingway or Steinbeck sharing a secret to literary genius that no professor was bold enough to provide.

Up to that point, I had smoked a modest amount of pot at a few parties, but never a cigarette. My parents, like most parents of their time, were avid smokers. My mom would smoke Virginia Slims, of course, and my dad was a two-pack-a-day Kent smoker. I had no desire for the side-effects: the permanent smell on clothes, cars, and living rooms; the yellow tinge on teeth and fingers; and the deep, wet cough that heavier smokers all have.

Then, there was the Debbie factor. Debbie was my first and only girlfriend who would soon become my wife. She came from a very religious family. Smoking and drinking violated their covenants with the Almighty, so there was no talk or tempt of the better vices of life. However, Debbie went to college in Missouri five hours away, so if I only had one cigarette with Brad, I could explain it as college experimentalism—a successful strategy nearly every college student has employed to cure or succumb to their curiosity of those things never discussed at the dinner tables of decent people.

Faced with the choice of discovering the secret to literary genius, the scorn of a girlfriend five hours away who may never ask (and I'd never tell), and the deadline for my short story quickly approaching—the decision for a single dance with this mistress was a very easy one to make. I asked Brad if I could try one.

He pulled out the pack, tapped the bottom end hard three times against his palm as if he were awakening the power of a genie in a small paper pack, and shook the top so a single cigarette came to the opening of the pack. He held it out to me. I slowly pulled this particular Camel out, rolled it in my fingers for whatever reason I can't recall, and put it in my mouth. The flavor of an unlit cigarette with no filter is pure. It is as smooth as Earle Grey tea. Brad struck a match and held it to the cigarette as I awkwardly inhaled, fixated for some reason at the subtle crackling of the tobacco as the cigarette lit. It was the only sound I heard in an otherwise bustling campus crowd.

I inhaled and exploded with a deep, hard, uncontrolled cough.

Brad laughed a robust laugh and said, "Here, Rookie, let me show you how it's done."

THE LAST LETTER

"First, don't take a drag like you're sucking a golf ball through a garden hose. Go easy on it. Let the cig come to you, don't chase it.

"You're holding it like your choking your chicken. How you hold it depends on the task at hand. When you're writing hold hit between your index and middle finger, like this. That way you can take a drag without thinking about it, and flick the ashes easier."

I gazed as though I was getting my first lesson in proper lovemaking. He went on.

"In the heat of debate or periods of pensive thought, the thumb and index finger is the preferred stance so you can more easily discard the cigarette in contempt or roll it methodically as you focus on the thought of the moment. For more intense thought, the whole-hand to the mouth approach—with the cigarette held between any two of the four fingers--brings the attention solely on the cigarette and the soothing tobacco inside."

"Are there any other ways I should know about?"

"Jesus, Larry, you're not learning physics here. It's a cigarette. Trust me, you'll get the hang of it."

I wasn't sure I really wanted to get the hang of it, but I pressed on. After I learned the nuances of inhaling and holding, I was four comforting puffs in and didn't notice anything. No clarity. No deep, universal wisdom. Definitely no magic. I did not feel any differently, and the first, fresh puff was turning into a dry, dirty taste in my mouth—no smoker can recreate the taste of the first draw of a good cigarette, but they spend the rest of the smoke trying.

I started to reach down to put it out and Brad said,

"Give it two more draws. Take your time. Never rush a good smoke."

By that second draw I was committed. I had calm. I had clarity. I danced with the mistress and it felt very, very good. And, with every draw, the mistress looked more beautiful and I did not want the dance to end. "Damn. I get it." I said with a newfound coolness and ease of thought.

After I finished my first cigarette, I gave Brad a nod and a "Thanks for the smoke.", now that I felt like a member of the club. I sauntered back into the union and finished my short story in less than two hours—a record for me. The work, to this day, is one of the best things I have ever written.

The next day, I went to the grocery store for provisions and added a pack of Camel straights and matches to my detergent, food, and sundry. I decided I would only smoke one cigarette at a sitting so I would not get addicted—the irrational compromise every early addict makes; the deal with the devil. However, I stuck to it. It became part of the process, and the process—more than the nicotine—became the addiction.

Before I would start any writing assignment or even free writing which I often chose to do, I would tap the bottom of the pack three times very hard in my palm, pop one cigarette to the opening, and pull it out slowly, rolling it between my forefinger and thumb for a few seconds so I could admire the simple pleasure I was about to enjoy. After slowly bringing it to sit between my lips, I would savor it for five or ten seconds and then strike the match and light it. The sound and the smell of the first slow draw of a cigarette are far more satisfying than those that follow. The last draw and the hard tamp into the ashtray to put the cigarette out has always been nearly as satisfying for me because it reinforces my illusion of control. I do not "need" another cigarette and while I may want one, I have the power to resist. Until, on occasion, I don't.

A week went by with the postal bags and Camels quietly hiding from the world in the confines of my shop. After dinner that night, I asked Debbie to put the kids to bed because I was going to work in the shop for a bit before coming in myself. I sat at my desk for a few minutes to assure there would be no interruptions, nervous that I may possibly sit there for days and still not have any idea of what to do with the hidden bags and their undiscovered contents. Then, I pulled the top right drawer of my desk open and pulled out the cigarettes and matches. I tapped the pack, pulled out a single Camel, rolled it in my fingers, set it between my lips, and struck a match.

I did not touch the postal duffels. I did not move the rags and towels I had over them. I stared, shifting my focus from the bag, to my safe, to the shop window, and rolled my cigarette between my forefinger and thumb. My safe is a large, old cast-iron safe I bought at an estate sale, telling Debbie it would look cool in the shop, but knowing full well my intent for the purchase. I kept all my college writings and a few short stories in the safe. I am the only one with the combination. Every few years I open the safe to read through the weighty tomes, in part or whole, to remind me of a different person from a different time with different talents.

There was great weight in determining if this was even a journey I could take, regardless of whether I chose to or not.

Frankly, I have never considered myself a talented writer, and certainly not a brilliant writer. I graduated Magna Cum Laude with a B.A. in literature. I was a structurally proficient writer and had a strong sense of description. However, my writing lacked the deeper luminescence that can only be derived from either the darker places of a soul or hues of deep passion. While I had a passion for writing, my attempts to express the nuances of the human condition often seemed flat, even muted. Talented, gifted writers use the full spectrum of human color while my own writing seemed to be served only by primary colors, like a rainbow with faded hues.

My professors and classmates would comment on my detail and story integrity, but never the beauty of thought. I rarely let others read my work outside of class as I was fearful they would discover what I already knew—high grades aside, I wrote for the joy of writing rather than allowing the reader to find joy in what I wrote. It wasn't insecurity as much as self-awareness as a voracious reader myself.

I wrote non-fiction in intensely researched, methodical detail. I wrote mysteries and science fiction for different classes, receiving "A's" in all my efforts. I became aware of my shortcoming as I was assigned a short story regarding love. While I conveyed well-documented historical aspects of love, I was never able to draw from an inner passion to write about and personalize love. In four years of college, that assignment would be the only "B" that I received.

My concern was whether my friend had held false confidence in my ability to help tell his story. Would I be able to help my friend? Would I be able to empathize with his plight in such a way as to make sense of the desperate situation he found himself in and convey that situation with any meaningful significance? Before I could accept this assignment, I had to determine if I would have the wherewithal to do more than just transcribe the efforts of a dying man. He had trusted me with his last thoughts. He had trusted me to bring sense to a senseless situation, to find meaning and order in the path he chose.

There are twenty cigarettes in a pack of Camel straights, so I rationalized that I had twenty opportunities for clarity of purpose and direction. Each night I had a single cigarette, which takes around fifteen minutes if you savor it. I savored slowly enough to usually pull another five minutes out of each one. As the pack drew down I still had no answers, and certainly no clarity. Until Camel number sixteen. By the third slow and deliberate drag, it all became very clear to me.

I would do my research as a writer before curating any content. I would go through each envelope and parcel and sort them by date. I would re-create the journey without taking it so I could decide if, and when, I wanted to embark. I would organize the content, create structure, and allow the theme to present itself to me. Then, I would use the trust he had placed in me to supplant the lack of confidence I had in bringing the full spectrum of color to his very personal story.

I grabbed a notebook and a pencil and noticed my full palm bringing the cigarette to my mouth at a torrid pace as I outlined my plan. I had clarity. I had purpose. I had vision. The riddle of this burden was going to be solved and I had taken the first step—the hardest step. I abruptly put the cigarette out well before its statute of limitation, dumped the contents of the bag on the dusty, broken concrete floor of my shop, and covered it all with an old tarp. This would take time, and I had to get back into the house.

CHAPTER 4
MAPPING THE JOURNEY

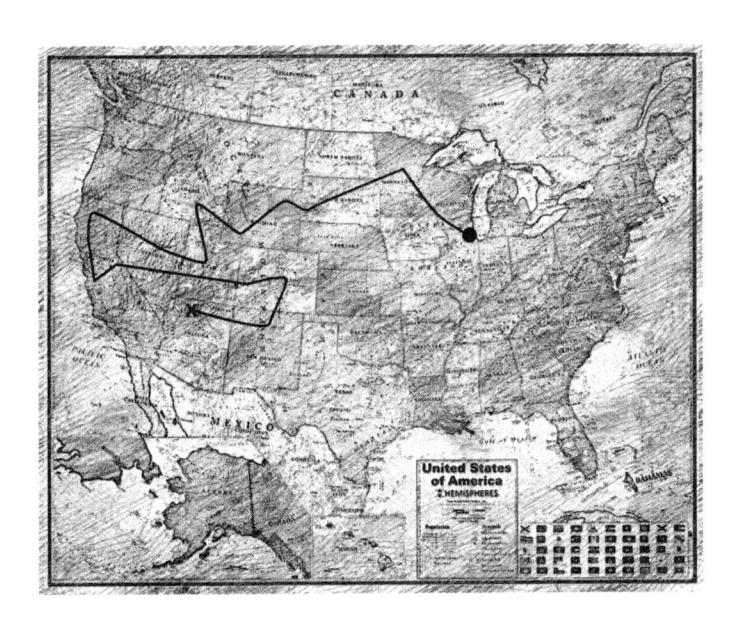

I mentioned to Debbie that I was going to start a work project Sunday afternoon in the shop. With small children, Saturdays are a mix of moment and mayhem where interruptions are the norm, the weekend "to-do" list is long, and the daylight is short. Debbie and I split the tasks at hand

and hope to accomplish whatever the day allows. Sundays are focused on church. Preparing the children for church. Attending church. Dinner with either side of the family after church. By mid-afternoon, Debbie and I both have a few hours to ourselves and take turns watching the kids while the other is afforded two to three hours of space and time for our own pursuits.

On Sunday, I approached the shop, looking from side to side to assure no one may be watching as I walked through, cognizant that our nearest neighbor is a quarter of a mile away. Once in the shop, I lit a cigarette, took a few draws, and let it sit on an old carburetor float bowl while I pulled away the tarp. I went through every letter and parcel, creating piles based on dates, then smaller piles as I fine-tuned the sequence of events of this journey of a dead friend. In all, there were 193 objects, now conveniently laid out on the floor in perfect sequence. I felt a sense of enormous accomplishment. However, I had not sensed that three hours had passed in my frenzy.

There was a knock on the shop door that startled me with that heavy, body-weakening pulse every conspirator must feel when they know they are on the cusp of getting caught. I went to the door and cracked it open--clearly the wrong response--as it solicited a look of modest suspicion from Debbie. I opened it wider and said, "Sorry about that, you surprised me."

"What you got going on in there? Something special?" Damn. She was onto me.

"Just wrapping up a work project and was caught off guard by the knock. Guess I got a little too into the project."

I immediately thought of my long extinguished single

THE LAST LETTER

cigarette and wondered if she would notice any lingering smoke.

"Dinner is ready," she said. "You've been out here quite a while. Must be a pretty big project for work."

"Oh," I replied, "I got stuck on the project so decided to do a little work on the mower engine and I guess time got by me trying to rebuild the carburetor." My story didn't even make sense to me, but she seemed to be pacified by the response.

She smiled and simply replied, "Okay. Time to wash up."

It was the first time in my life that I have lied to my wife and of greater concern was that it happened quickly, easily, and effectively. I paused and considered taking all of the letters and packages directly to our burn barrel before dinner so I would never have to experience the feeling of self-compromise I was feeling at that moment. Lying, like smoking, is an addiction that once started can never fully be controlled or extinguished. It is a clock that you can't unwind.

I turned to the long line of evidence, sorted sequentially like a well-diagrammed crime scene in a yet unsolved mystery, and decided that throwing the tarp back over the material was not the most noble act, but it was the most expedient. I went inside, washed my hands, and sat down to dinner with my family. I had a sense of confidence and satisfaction I hadn't had for quite some time, and I hoped it wasn't visible.

I waited a few days to let any consequences of my Sunday session play out, and was thankful that there were none. After I put the kids to bed, I mentioned I was going to get back on that work project in the shop for an hour or so. I learned my lesson, so I took an old cooking alarm from the kitchen out to the shop the day before, set the time, and allowed myself no more than forty-five minutes to continue so I had enough time to conceal the artifacts of my increasingly critical mission before going back in the house.

With the sequence of events clearly in front of me, I began writing the postmark date, location, and any other visible clues from each letter, parcel, and package. While thorough, it did not provide the perspective I needed before I would begin the more labored task of connecting time to place, content to context.

A few days later, I went to the Ben Franklin in Knoxville on my way home from work and purchased a large corkboard and a map of the United States that would fit within it. For added measure, I also purchased colored pins, not knowing if I would really need them or not. And, some paste. I did not know what I would or would not need, but I did know that in order to proceed on this clandestine path I would only have one or two opportunities to purchase anything and deliver it safely to the shop without being discovered. By this time, I was too far in to risk discovery. I was fortunate that Debbie, a third-grade teacher at our local elementary, had conferences that night, allowing me a free pass with my supplies into the shop.

I pasted the map to the cork board and referred to my worksheet to chart the dates and places Tracy had gone. I used a felt marker to note the date by each town and placed a blue pin if that location corresponded to a letter, a red pin for a package, and a black pin for a box. Every other night over the course of the week I continued to chart the sequence of events that led to my friend's passing. I put a large black dot on Chicago to note the beginning of the end and a large, black "X" in Kayenta, Arizona where I assume the end occurred.

I had a great sense of accomplishment and satisfaction. It was worthy of celebration, so I did what I cannot recall ever doing before—I had a second cigarette, drawing it with my full palm fast and frequently, and stared at the map as I leaned back confidently in my chair with my feet propped up on the desk. By the final draw, I knew I was ready to begin the journey to find out how my friend lived and how he died. I slept as hard and sound that night as I ever have in my entire life.

The next day at work I began to think about my approach. The precision of my approach gave me a sense of energy I had not felt in quite some time, energy derived from a sense of purpose and path for a once unsolvable problem. Sitting alone over a cup of stale, black coffee in the V.A. break room that morning, I realized that this energy had no circuit—no path to regulate or direct the current. I was so relieved to get to my starting point that I neglected the minutia necessary to sustain it.

I needed method and boundaries if I had any chance of moving this forward with my newfound energy. The details came quite quickly, actually, and seemed basic enough that I wouldn't need to write them down:

1. I would limit my visits to the shed to no more than one hour per session, both to allow me to walk away from the project and to keep any suspicion from arising at home.

2. I would only attempt two sessions during the week, interspersed with an hour actually working on something in the shop—anything that would put grease on my hands or sawdust on my clothes to better avoid detection. If life allowed for additional time on a Sunday, I would use it, but I would not let this become a distraction from my responsibilities as a father and a husband.
3. I would read as much as possible in the first thirty minutes so I could use the second half of the hour to chronicle the content.
4. I would never read out of sequence out of respect for my friend and the story he chose to tell.
5. I would never—EVER—have a second cigarette again. Too noticeable. Loss of control and discipline, and both would be needed to succeed.
6. Always leave no trace. I would spend the last few minutes of each hour hiding the evidence, including my notes, the letters and packages, and especially any spent cigarette butts and matches.

By the end of my break, there was one looming question remaining. Would I tell Debbie and—if so—when and how would be the best way to approach her? I had already accomplished enough in this coffee break to decide that it was best I leave a question with such levity for another day. I had patients to work with and a few minutes' walk back to the industrial therapy building to help me transition to reality.

CHAPTER 5

THE LIFE, AS I KNOW IT, OF TRACY MCGUIRE

Before I opened the first envelope, I felt it worthy to reflect on my experience and perceptions of Tracy from the time we met until my last interaction with him a few years before his letter arrived. It would also help remind me of the reference points of his correspondence. Framing who he was and who he is may better help me better understand what he was going through.

I met Tracy McGuire on the first day of school in sixth grade. He had moved to Pleasantville from Arizona the summer before and noticeably stuck out because in a town our size the average graduation class is around fifty, and our class was one of the smaller classes with just forty-one. A full thirty-eight of the forty-one of us had started school together in kindergarten. In a small town, even if you moved to town in third grade, upon your graduation you still won't be considered "from here". And, if you moved here with no relatives in the area you definitely weren't "from here". Fortunately for the McGuire family, there were relatives in town—cousins—and therefore a point of reference for fellow students.

Tracy was the youngest of three children who lived with his mother in Tracy's maternal grandparents' home after his parents were divorced in Phoenix. His older brother, Tom, was in the grade ahead of us and his older sister, Katie, had the greatest challenge of all coming into the small, tight circle of her high school class four years ahead of us as a sophomore—a definite outsider with only three years to learn the structure, mores, and background of her classmates prior to graduation.

On Tracy's first day it was obvious his strategy was to parlay the relative romance of his transfer from an exotic locale like Arizona to a small town in Iowa into credibility with his classmates, particularly the girls as if he was born on the great mesas of the Grand Canyon—the only reference point any of us had about Arizona. Regardless of your credentials, trying to jump ahead in the pecking order of middle school is strictly forbidden, and he learned that quickly. He wasn't from here. He would probably leave here sooner than later. He didn't yet know his place. He was also one of the smallest students in our grade—boy or girl—which didn't help his cause.

He compensated for his small stature with an abundance of personality. He talked more than anyone else in our class and had a great deal of charm and affability. Some students are shy, and some are approachable but do not initiate conversation. Tracy was the kind of student that approached everyone—a busy bee flying from flower to flower regardless of the size and shape of the petals. His size taught him to be a threat to no one and in those rare cases that he was, to talk his way out of the thickest of situations.

In a strange twist of sibling irony, his older brother was his exact opposite. Tom was quiet. Reserved. He was also very big—one of the biggest kids in the class above us. He didn't need the Arizona passport to find his place in the pecking order—in junior high school, size and strength for boys determine your place in line, your challengers, and the width of your wake as you walk the halls. If you are quiet with any hint of a scowl you move up in that order more quickly.

The difference in size and personality was noticeable and immediate. In small-town schools, teachers understand and reinforce the pecking order and would comment—rarely kindly--as often as the students on the difference in size and substance of both of the brothers.

The explanation was detailed by Tracy in another attempt at new kid credibility. He was smart—he started school in second grade when he was five years old after skipping both kindergarten and first grade. He was the youngest student in junior high—in fact, for both years that he was in junior high he was the youngest student. Tom, on the other hand, had been held back a year in grade school so they were a year apart in school, three years apart in age, and worlds apart in appearance and demeanor.

Junior high is famously brutal. Closeness in a class of forty-one is forged from universal contempt. Any perception--real or created—of imperfection or difference that can be announced and exploited will be used against you in the court of social status. Dodging daily verbal and, occasionally, physical barbs were the norm and allowed every student to hone their skills in attack, retreat, and surrender that would serve as worthy strategies in the larger arena of high school.

In junior high, Tracy was noticeably bright, yet with no focus or discipline and a penchant for interruption and distraction. In the early '80s, corporal punishment was the discipline of choice for most educators so several times a week we were witness to Tracy getting Mr. Hancock's paddle at the front of math class for talking to others during the lesson. Or, the assignment of writing the longest word in the English language—pneumonoultramicroscopicsilicovolcanoconiosis—fifty times in cursive overnight to avoid detention the next day in Mrs. Hildman's English class. We all were familiar with that word by the end of junior high, but few students had it indelibly embedded into their psyche like Tracy. His hand had gained muscle memory and he could write the word fifty times blindfolded.

Our passage to high school was simple. Physically, the junior high and senior high were in the same building. And, since most of our older siblings, cousins, parents, and grandparents had gone to school in the same building, there was no lack of familiarity.

Tracy had refined his charm as we progressed through high school, but his penchant for disruption also continued to flourish. It was a training ground for him—he flirted with minor misdeeds seemingly for the challenge of either minimizing the damage or avoiding it altogether. As he grew into his charm, his confidence also continued to grow. Some teachers responded positively to his ways, yet most had very little time for someone who tried to talk his way into and out of the regiment required in class.

It is common knowledge that high school is nothing more than an assembly of tribes—nation-states of social status. The most powerful, and the most popular, are the athletes. Then, there are the intellects—those focused on a future dependent upon classroom achievement. The artists—band, choir, and drama—are generally more tightly knit, bound by their subtle disdain for athletes and their enjoyment for the more creative expressions of life. The final group is the less recognized—kids of divorced parents, welfare kids, "potheads", and trouble-makers. While the other "nations" have common boundaries, this last group is more like an island separated from the others with restricted travel to and from the group.

One would think in a typical class of forty to fifty students, these groups wouldn't be as distinct as in larger high schools, but it's just the opposite. While many students may have citizenship in more than one of the countries, the community, and the educators are quick to help frame the home country for nearly every student. For example, an athlete may be smart, and may join the choir, but they are still "a jock" and treated like a visitor—sometimes welcome, and sometimes not--when they venture out of their pre-determined social association.

Tracy was a man without a "country". I don't believe it was by choice. It certainly was not due to disrespect for the long-honored rules of clique inclusion. He just did not seem to know any better—he was naïve. He was an athlete, but certainly not the high-caliber sort. He was smart, but not disciplined enough to be welcomed by the intellectuals. He was a singer much more in spirit than talent. He excelled in drama but had great disregard for the theatre crowd. As a child of modest means and a non-traditional living arrangement, he could identify with the "islanders" but tried to avoid any perception of residency in that outer limit.

He committed the cardinal sin of high school hierarchy—he attempted friendship with members of every group which excluded him from the rights of full-time residency in any one. Each "country" maintains covalent bonds of friendship that are exclusive to "residents" and friendships outside of your respective clique had consequences—once you are exiled, no efforts of conformity will allow you to return.

His closest attempt was his relationship with Rhonda Myers, a very popular girl two grades below us. It was common for high school boys to find affection in younger girls, although those courtships can only take place once both are in high school. Dating a junior high girl when you are in high school was strictly frowned upon, even if it was a relationship carried over from junior high. It was as if there was an imaginary boundary in the building, a line that cannot be crossed.

They became a couple toward the end of our junior year, and the relationship provided status legitimacy that he may not have otherwise found. They were together until early in our sophomore year in college when the difference in who he was in high school and who he was becoming in college--who he realized he wanted to be--created more weight than the relationship could bear.

One of the seminal moments for the two McGuire boys happened our freshman year. Both chose wrestling over basketball, a decision most young Iowa males choose to make very early in life. Tom, then a sophomore, was wrestling heavyweight. He was light for a heavyweight but strong and large enough to earn the status. Tracy wrestled at 105 pounds, the second lightest weight class. In what would be Tracy's first varsity match and Tom's last, his brother broke his collarbone in a match against a true heavyweight.

After that, Tom had moved from top-tier athlete clique toward the bottom, never wrestling again and with diminished interest in athletics, choosing instead to live on the island in the realm of the pot smokers and low aspirations and expectations afforded to those around him. As Tracy grew and became more athletic, and therefore more popular and confident, he climbed toward the boundaries of the top group but never held a place within it. In college, when we would talk about family, he would often reference that wrestling meet as the event that turned their respective differences in personality and demeanor into completely different paths in life. His observation appeared to be correct.

Every smalltown high school student approaches graduation with one of three very distinct paths firmly in mind. There are those that plan to work in the area, just as their parents and grandparents before them have done. There are those that choose to go to college or the military to decide what they would like to pursue and where before returning back home. Finally, there are those that plan to leave—typically for college—with no plans to ever return... the "get the hell out of here and never look back" group. He was in the last group and at our graduation party expressed more relief than most that the chapter was closed and would never be read again.

Tracy and I both attended college thirty miles away at Central College, a small liberal arts school. One of my best friends from high school, David Wayne, joined us; he and I were roommates. I chose to attend to pursue my passion for literature. David chose to be anywhere but Pleasantville and investigate psychology. Tracy attended to be close enough to the comfort of his high school girlfriend, yet far enough away to remove the social shackles that bound him in high school. After wandering through pre-law, then theatre, he finally settled on the rather generic degree of communications. We each had different motives for our move and a new world in which to explore them.

College provided a new audience: each student thankful for the opportunity to share their history with others while creating their history on a new page each day. It also provided a broader range of interests to explore, and more expertise from those leading the exploration. And, of course, it provided alcohol and vices of various sorts outside the watchful eyes of parents and community.

I remained comfortably introverted with a close yet expanding circle of friends and trusted acquaintances. I was a member of the band and concert choir, in addition to my studies and trips home to spend time with Debbie. It was a reasonable balance of familiar and new, and I found comfort in both.

David flourished, creating constraint-free friendships with people he found of interest or hobby. He elected to be as introverted or extroverted as the situation offered. He, more than most, enjoyed the newfound freedom of defining who he was and who he wished to be, on his terms, at his pace. He joined the cross-country team, although he never ran in high school. He also surprised us, and possibly himself, by joining the same fraternity Tracy was in—the Thetas--opting to pledge as an upper-classman. David used our four years at Central to broaden his experience base and was quite brave in tasting everything on the menu without fear, yet seldom without risk.

Tracy chose to play football, noting to David and me that he had "unfinished business" on the field. He was still the youngest student in college until our junior year, and while he had grown physically, a sixteen-year-old freshman playing college football ended up finishing that "business" in a brutal fashion. He was obsessed to succeed and spent every day opting out of class for time in the gym. By the end of our freshman year, he had returned to Pleasantville for summer as a very muscular and confident young man. That confidence and physique still covered the emotional soul and simplicity of a teenager.

Tracy's sister, Katie, attended Central and he didn't as much follow in her footsteps as trample them like a wild bull. She had established a reputation as a good student and good person, majoring in psychology and playing softball. He had no intention of settling for younger brother status to a solid collegiate citizen and by the end of our freshman year was an audacious, obnoxious star attraction at upper-class parties, which caused visible disdain from Katie and the four years of legacy building she had hoped to maintain. He was not harming her legacy as younger siblings can occasionally do. He was dimming it, which is far more difficult for a senior sibling to accept.

There was a simple pureness to Tracy in college and it was derived from a genuinely uncommon lack of awareness of both his gifts and his liabilities. In his mind, he just "was". As an observer, I can attest that he was gravity without mass. He could be obnoxious, even boorish, in both word and deed. Yet he could be kind and thoughtful. He would showcase world-class narcissism, modesty, and diffidence, often in the same conversation. He could relate to nearly anyone, yet could act as if he cared for no one, certainly not himself or his self-preservation. He was driven to impress—in the moment, rather than through a body of work--with mixed success.

Tracy was unpredictable. The only constant was his sole focus on the moment, rather than any attention that might come from it. He was unaware of all this and had no desire to understand lest he miss the next moment and the anxious anticipation for something extraordinary to happen.

For some college students, alcohol relaxes inhibitions. For Tracy alcohol was like jet fuel for a rudderless rocket.

THE LAST LETTER

No one wanted to miss the launch and everyone wanted to witness the crash and there was ample opportunity for both. There was the night a fraternity party crowd seemed to thin out. When I was leaving, I noticed the crowd had gone outside where Tracy was spitting in the air and catching it back in his mouth while onlookers bet on each launch like it was Russian Roulette—the first miss was painful to watch. Or when David dared him to scale to the top of our three-story dormitory and back down after the bar closed. There were plenty of bar fights that he would either start and not finish or try to finish once others had started.

None of us were without our quirks, and Tracy was no different. Any moment was turned into a competition, and the more obtuse, the better. Who could throw a ball closest to the ceiling without touching it. Who could fully recite the label of a Budweiser bottle blindfolded. Ginger versus Mary Ann from Gilligan's Island (still an eternal question with no clear answer). Who could keep a pillow feather in the air the longest. Who could break the most pencils across a single finger. All the contests were for a dollar that was usually left unpaid by the end. The competition, not the prize, seemed to be what he yearned for—and that yearning was a constant in his life and demeanor.

He had an uncanny memory and could recite scenes from any movie from the past decade or lyrics from most songs. Music, television, and movies were his metaphorical reference for nearly every situation and he mixed lines and verses into most conversations. He was obsessed with trivial facts, and the more inane the information was, the better. He could try to fascinate with the top five potato-producing countries in the world, or the last number-one single of Elvis

Presley. All the information was delivered with both context and curiosity.

There was also the word "fuck", which he expelled with poetic abundance. He could use it as a noun, verb, pronoun, adverb, and adjective and occasionally did so within the same sentence. His most famous quote came in an intramural softball game against the rival fraternity, the Phi Betas. According to David, in the late innings of a particularly tough drubbing at the hands of the Betas, he stormed into the dugout and yelled at his Theta teammates, "Fuck! I am so fucking tired of losing to the Phi fucking Betas, so you fucking fuckballs better stop playing like such a big pile of fuck or I'll personally beat your fucking asses with a bat. You ever been bat-fucked? You won't fucking like it." There were different versions carried forward in recants, but the soliloquy was recited by others often for years. When presented with the damning evidence at parties or in conversation, his only reply was, "Well, it was true." He was the Ernest Hemingway of the f-bomb.

He was not a committed student but still graduated with honors. He had absolutely no scholastic grit and would typically put in the work the week before finals and wait with a great deal of angst to see his grades after each semester. He was a class master, engaging in dialogue and debate with professors when he did attend class. While that elevated his grades with some professors, more were quick to approach him with stern lectures on underachievement. As a student sharing a lecture hall with him, I can confirm that he was easy to dislike.

And, there were women. Shortly before, and very likely because, Rhonda Myer broke up with him at the beginning

THE LAST LETTER

of our sophomore year he realized he was no longer in a small town; no longer bound by the rules of relationships, and he had a wide field of opportunity—like a wolf in the middle of a herd of elk. He had many overnight guests.

A small college is like a small town, however, and a reputation for very short-term relationships with the opposite sex travels fast and without mercy. By the end of our sophomore year, he was labeled as a "womanizer" which meant any decent-minded, self-respecting young woman would and should give him no mind or matter, or if they did it would only be done in the quiet dignity of darkness.

He discussed this during one night of heavy drinking and heavier conversation in our dorm room and expressed great frustration by the label. There was a disconnect between his actions and the consequences. He was naïve and combative. He didn't wear his reputation as a badge of machismo honor around those he trusted with his thoughts, opting instead for disbelief and denial. His irrational rationale was that if they came to his room, they should carry the scarlet letter rather than him. He mentioned a few of the names—many good Christian girls—and made a convincing yet defeated argument.

He and David studied together in Mexico for the first semester of our sophomore year. They roomed together and, as David described it, became closer by disavowing the contempt that each had held toward the other from membership in different high school cliques, even though I do not recall either of them belonging to any one group exclusively. They chose to create a new history bound by the desire to disregard their respective pasts. Although they returned with a closer friendship, there was still a subtle tension between them that I would not fully understand until we were nearing graduation. Upon their return, Tracy started to play rugby on the local college team and seemed to have found the outlet for his "unfinished business" of football. He continued to play during college, a year in Europe for a club team, then several years with a team in Chicago after graduation.

In our junior year, he and David both studied in Britain during the second semester. He had broken up with his placeholder girlfriend at the beginning of school, vowing to remain unattached before leaving overseas. Love is not convenient, however, and within a few weeks of breaking up, he met and quickly fell as deeply in love as a young man can be with Kristen Johnson. Kristen was a quiet, attractive young woman in the class below us and the two were inseparable until his flight abroad. His plan of studying abroad unattached had failed. Based on letters from David, he had also failed to be faithful to Kristen while he was overseas which created heated battles between David and Tracy on values, morals, and the true meaning of committed love. Battles that neither would win, but battles fought for the good of the fight.

Kristen studied abroad her junior year in Paris as Tracy returned to campus for our senior year. While he still vowed a love deeper than others could possibly understand, our senior year was his most prolific in terms of various female companions. The deep disparity in his words and actions relating to women was the source of several interventions by his—and Kristen's—well-minded friends. The irony was that a few of those well-minded friends were also frequent paramours.

THE LAST LETTER

The topic of Tracy and his contradictions came up often in late-night conversation among friends that knew we were from the same town and had remained friends. Most of our more refined friends thought he was an obnoxious ass with limited intellect and even lower values, but admitted he was fun to watch—from a safe distance. One of our close friends, Karen Gleason, summed it up well one cannabis-assisted evening. "He is so damn lovable when you talk to him, but he fucks-up. A lot. He's the forbidden fruit. Any good Christian girl knows he won't change—the sin will always follow the first bite of that apple."

He had become a student ambassador for the admissions department. He could excite a potential student on the frivolity provided by the college experience while somehow convincing the parents that the college would provide strict guardianship and Christian values over their children while they attended. His hyperbole—his lies—in both cases worked. He was quick to point out he had the highest "close rate" of any member of the admissions team and that he could play a parent like a grand piano and direct any personality type of prospective student like the conductor of a marching band. He could sell.

Toward the end of our senior year, there was one event late in the evening during the week of finals where I witnessed a defining moment between Tracy and David that resonates with me to this day. We were in the campus library in the 24-hour study room. Our best attempts to study for finals eventually led to cheap tequila shots from a flask David had with him. As with most nights of similar course between the two, David and Tracy had a contest to see who had the courage and talent to jump from the highest of thirty steps of the grand staircase leading from the ground floor of the library to the main floor. It was a contest between the two that several of us had witnessed before, but I was the only audience member for this final collegiate challenge.

One would start at the first step with a small jump, then the other would have to follow. With each higher step came greater risk, like playing H-O-R-S-E in basketball but with the loser either acknowledging defeat before their turn to jump or breaking an ankle. At the start of the seventeenth step—just over halfway to the top and a fifteen-foot fall—David stopped and looked directly at Tracy and said, "You know we all hate you."

Tracy laughed and said, "Fuck you."

David did not flinch and replied, "I'm serious. We all hate you."

The contest, and the world, stopped immediately and changed course with a far more serious tone. When Tracy asked why, David said, "You don't even try. People are naturally drawn to you and you don't even care. You have no idea how hard we have to work for something that you were born with. You shit on the gift of charisma that God gave you."

Tracy looked down at me from the seventeenth step and asked if I felt the same way.

"Hate is a strong word, Tracy," was all I could say.

"Everyone?" he asked.

"Everyone that knows you well enough to care," I sheepishly replied.

"I didn't ask for it. The charisma," he said, as if to feign awareness, but not acknowledge it. He stared down the stairs and into the distance, then back to David and I.

THE LAST LETTER

"If people hate me for it, how good of a gift can it be?" I do not recall what happened after that statement, but I know we never spoke of that night, or that topic, ever again.

A week later we graduated. I still have the picture of David and Tracy after the ceremony. They both agreed to wear a dress shirt and tie under their gown, and nothing else. In the picture, they were arm in arm with their gowns unzipped and a full-frontal view of their semi-exposed selves. I am sure they didn't realize the metaphorical value of the pose at the time.

There was one thing that was clear to me by the time we graduated to become full-time working adults. There are those—like me—that prefer the view from the bleachers and the relative security it offers to observe and participate as active, interested bystanders. For others, the arena is the only place they can exist, often not by choice.

They need the arena, not for the spectators but for the dirt and the sweat, for the challenge and the immediacy of outcomes: success or failure, strength or injury, exhilaration or defeat, pride or shame. They prefer the arena, whether for practice or match. They have no desire to learn life lessons from the wider lens afforded to those in the stands. There have always been and will always be more spectators in the stands than performers in the arena. Tracy was destined for a life in the arena as if it was a curse rather than a choice.

College concluded with added self-awareness for my friend, but—for reasons I do not know—he still seemed somewhat developmentally disabled, naïve to the structure of the world and his place in it. It was as if he had found bits and pieces of himself without knowing just where the pieces of the puzzle should fit to create a clear picture of himself.

After graduation, Tracy cast a broad net looking for a job anywhere but Iowa and found employment in Chicago at an advertising agency. He started, as he'd say, "As close to the mail room as you can get without opening envelopes."

He began as a copy writer and seemed to progress quickly, but was quick to point out that his job was a means to an end—he noted that he spent every spare moment and every available dollar playing rugby around the country and pursuing his passion for adventure focusing on mountaineering and rock climbing. The stories of his travels—both for work and play--were luminous.

He came home a few times a year those first few years and would always call a few of us to meet at the North End, the smaller of the two taverns in town. It is a converted gas station with three small tables and no more than ten well-worn, often unoccupied, stools around the bar at any given time. The North End sits on the edge of town and is known for two things—the transition point between factory jobs in Des Moines and home for heavier drinkers, and the weekend gathering place for those that have left town to come back and connect with their former friends. The added benefit: they sell beer for carry-out after the convenience store closes at eleven.

During his visits, we would talk about our lives, past, and current. Clocks tick slower in a small town and calendars blur from one year to the next. Like the town, the lives of its inhabitants do not change much, so the talk often drifted toward questions of, and elaborate responses regarding, Tracy's conquests—the city, a long list of women within it, his travels, and his experiences on different mountains and rivers in the Americas and Africa.

THE LAST LETTER

The North End was typically the start of night, and where it would end, how, and with whom, were always questions that only the brave or uninitiated would stay to answer. If you did not go home after the North End, you were assured to be a player in a story to be shared for months after his departure.

One year around Christmas, several of us met at the North End as a heavy snow started to fall. Around midnight, and well after I had promised Debbie I would be home, Tracy convinced me, two of our classmates, and Jolene Parker—an attractive girl four years our junior—to buy a case of carryout beer and drive around town in the heavy snow as if we were in a demolition derby with a much larger figure eight-track. We spun through every road and parking lot at high speeds and low control. It was one of the wildest experiences of my life. It was as if there were no rules and no boundaries for around an hour. Until the lights came on.

As we were spinning "donuts" in the high school parking lot, we caught the less-than-watchful eye of Pete Spaulding, the single town law enforcement officer. Pete had a penchant for finding underage drinkers, stopping them, and--with the threat of incarceration or loss of license--absconding with their alcohol and letting them go. It was a fair trade in the spirit of "protect and serve"—he would protect your reputation, and you would serve him your beer.

On this particular night, his lights brought the car to a stop. He came upon the car and Tracy rolled his window down, preparing for the beer confiscation negotiation that was bound to occur. Unfortunately, one of our friends, Mike Mott, was in no mood to give up the rest of our beer, or the fun we were having. He threw empty beer cans out the window at Pete and yelled, "Leave us alone, Pete. And, you ain't touching our beer!"

The wildest time of my life quickly turned into the most frightening as Pete drew his service revolver from his holster, pointed it in the car, cocked the hammer, and responded, "Goddammit, Mott, you throw one more can and I'm pulling the trigger!"

I was in the passenger seat in the front, convinced we were all going to die, and realized at that moment that I made a very, very poor decision in not returning home after the North End. Tracy raised his hands and calmly said, "Pete, you're full within your rights to shoot that dumb sombitch, but if you do I'll never get the blood stains out of my car. How about we split what's left with you so you can un-cock that bad boy and we call it a night?"

Pete did un-cock his pistol but kept it pointed in the car. He looked back at Tracy and it turned into an everyday conversation:

"You staying at Grandma Bea's?"

"Yeah, I came home for Christmas."

"How's she doing with the cancer?"

"She's a fighter. We all have good hope."

"What the hell you doing out here?"

"It was snowing hard and looked like too much fun to pass up. Plus, I think they over-served us a little at the North End and we got a little ahead of ourselves."

"Tends to happen."

Pete told us to give him his half of the beer and told Tracy he'd follow us to his grandma's house, warning that if he saw us on the road after that, he'd have to take us to "county". There was no jail in Pleasantville, so serious offenders had to be taken to the county seat of Knoxville eleven miles away to spend the night in the county jail.

Pete followed us three blocks down State Street to Tracy's house—with the lights on, but no siren—and made sure we got out of the car and into the house before pulling out of the driveway to enjoy his beer before his shift ended. When we walked into the house, Tracy's brother, Tom, was in the living room with a large cafeteria tray stacked with marijuana that he was sorting, de-seeding, and bagging in plastic bags for future sale. He looked at us and said, "Why'd you bring the cops to the house, Budddd?"

Tracy just laughed and asked why he brought the opium den home for the holidays. I found myself in a crazy place, with crazy people, and a deep desire for the evening to end.

There was still the issue of how we would get home. The North End was only a few blocks straight down State Street, so three of us walked to our cars wondering what in God's name had just happened. Tracy told us he was going to take Jolene, whose parents lived a couple of miles west of town, home. We reminded him of Pete's warning and he reminded us that Pete was probably a few beers in by then and would have no appetite to drive him to Knoxville to process him at the county jail. He had a point, and—I am assuming—finished the night getting better acquainted with Jolene.

In the months after that visit, Tracy's grandma's cancer grew much worse. He came home more often, stayed longer, but rarely ventured far from home, and would rarely call to meet any of us. When he did, he clearly had the weight of imminent loss on his mind so the visits were brief and subdued.

That fall she passed away. We attended her funeral with many of our classmates. Tracy didn't—couldn't—say a word to any of us. He cried the entire service, left the church without speaking to any of his friends, hugged his family, and immediately drove back to Chicago, refusing to attend the graveside internment. The death of a parent creates a wound that, over time, heals leaving a scar of varying length and depth. In Tracy's case, the death of a parent acquired later in life left a wound that would never heal, and that he would never forgive.

With no home left in his "hometown", Tracy did not visit again for a few years. He did come back once, for the funeral of one of our classmates who had died returning home from work at the hands of a drunk driver. He came to the funeral in an expensive suit and had very clearly been urbanized. He was much more polished, although he still cursed like a drunken sailor. A few of our friends gave him grief for his "Wall Street" look and reminded him that he was home and he should be more mindful of that.

After the service, we ended up at the North End. We were sharing stories of days of old, catching up on the news of families and friends, and asking Tracy about his latest adventures. Unlike previous visits, he was quick to defer to our stories, our adventures, however parochial they may have been. And, he seemed genuinely interested. He had changed, but the more we drank, the more we prodded him to find his old self. His stories, told in varying degrees of embellishment I'm sure, flowed seamlessly from one to the next.

After several rounds, more stories, and abundant laughter, one of the patrons in the corner stool of the bar,

Richard Gillihan—a regular at the North End, and self-anointed community leader who was much older than us—walked the three or four steps to our table and looked at Tracy and said, "Do you remember me?"

Tracy responded, "Of course, Richard. How are you doing?"

Richard drunkenly replied, "I don't know what you're doing now, but I can tell from the way you talk and the way you dress that it's something big."

Tracy seemed pleased and politely said in a drunken twang, "Well thank you, Richard."

Before another word could be said, Richard aggressively asserted, "Anybody that knew you growing up would be surprised, because nobody thought you'd amount to piss!"

Tracy finished more drunken fights than he started so he never turned down an invitation to a brawl, and this was clearly an invitation to settle a dispute of pride and perception. It was like a scene in an old western movie. We slowly backed away from the table; we had become accustomed to what happened next, and no one wants to be mistakenly drawn into the middle of a mean-spirited melee where insult begets injury.

But what happened next did not happen next. Tracy slowly and deliberately stood up, faced off, and smiled and said, "Well, to be honest, Richard, I guess it's surprised you and me both. What are you drinking tonight?"

Richard, taken noticeably off guard, stuttered and said, "Vodka on the rocks."

Tracy ordered his drink, shook his hand, and said it was nice to see him again. Richard returned to his stool and his vodka rocks and Tracy sat back down to our table to a group of dumbfounded stares. "What the fuck are y'all looking at?" he asked. "There's no win in kickin' Richard Gillihan's ass. Not tonight anyway."

Something had changed in our friend and we all noticed it, even if he had not. We were anticipating "the moment"—the creation of a story that would be recounted the next day and the next days after that. But Tracy opted for the richer, deeper, conversation with old friends that you never remember in topic, but endures far longer than a quick and decisive battle at the bar. Time, distance, and success had allowed Tracy to finally feel at home in a hometown he would ultimately never return to after that evening.

CHAPTER 6
THE FIRST LETTER

I had successfully charted the journey without opening an envelope. With the navigation firmly identified, it was time to discover. It was time to not just map the journey but take it.

After a deep drag from my Camel, I opened the first

envelope. It was dated April 4th and mailed from Chicago, Illinois. I removed the contents—a three-page hand-written letter written in small, but legible cursive. The contents of the first letter:

Dear Larry,

Jesus, what a night. And a morning. I have a world fucking class hangover and am surprised I'm not dead. Seriously, if the last 14 hours couldn't kill me, I doubt cancer can. The going-away party checked every box. Alcohol. Cocaine. Weed. Insanity. And, thanks to the cocktail of premium narcotics I got laid twice, the first time with an ex-girlfriend and her mom. How fucking epic is that?! A threesome with Leslie and Denise Brown. Kink factor: 9. Good to know I'm still very limber. The second time wasn't my best effort, but it was around 4 in the morning so I'm sure it will be easy to forget for both of us—my first ginger, by the way, so I was finally able to get past that phobia.

The cops came around two, not long after my recliner went out the window of my loft. Glad I wasn't in it, but there were chants that made it a closer call than it should have been. I bet everyone that I could get duct-taped in the chair and thrown through the window without dying. Lost my balls about halfway through the tape and got out, so we did a test run with the chair. God, drunks are fun. Rugby drunks, funner yet. Coked up drunks of any kind, the most fun. And, yep, that chair drop woulda killed me sure as shit.

I made my announcement around 10. I was leaving for a job overseas for three years. Chance of a lifetime, I said. Made a few special shoutouts, gave a few special things to a few special people and told everyone that we were to leave it all on the field—drink every drop, take every pill, smoke anything handed to them. Most important: leave nothing but stories. Based on how trashed my place is, the mob took every word to heart. Guess I won't get my security deposit back. Fuck the landlord. I will only miss the large Pleasantville road sign I stole with Troy Bennet one drunken winter night on Highway G40 during college. Sometimes, you can't take even the best memories with you.

I've spent the last few days prepping. Takes more thought to die than you'd expect. I went to REI to get some cold-weather gear for riding, a few camp supplies, and a new climbing harness and daisy chain. You give me a daisy chain, a few carabiners, and a good harness and there's not much I can't climb up or rappel down. I'm packing light. A few changes of clothes. A solo tent and sleeping bag. Hunting knife for close calls. Flashlight. Old Style beer cap—who wouldn't want to die in an Old Style cap? Riding gloves. I jigsaw puzzled all this into the side cases on my bike and used the trunk for my satchel.

From your vantage point, the satchel is the key. I have a few notepads, pens and pencils, a lot of envelopes and stamps, and a camera so I can send a few pictures. I also scored a cool mini-recorder and a box of cassettes in case I get tired of writing—plus, talking is much easier. Throw a wad of cash and checkbook in there for good measure and I'm about set.

The toughest task was picking no more than five CD's for my Sony Discman. Music's a big deal when you live, and I figure when you die, so I went through my whole library—over 500 discs—to pick just the right mix. Took me hours. I settled on U2's Joshua Tree—the best album ever. Thought about Abbey Road instead, but I'm convinced Joshua Tree will take its place as the best album ever—good to be ahead of the curve.

Had to have the Stones, so I picked Let It Bleed. Check track 9. You'll understand. Thought real hard about Rolling Stones in Mono just for "Sympathy with the Devil", but needed more juice.

Considered Johnny Cash At Folsom Prison, but decided on Waylon Jennings' Greatest Hits. A definite must. A ritual album I played in a hot bubble bath after every rugby tournament since forever with my cowboy hat on and a giant wad of Levi Garret in my cheek. Didn't get out until every song played. Waylon helped soothe every scrape and scratch, bruise and break, and several sprains. When the going does get tough, Waylon will take care of me. Always has.

Thought real hard about Wham! Make It Big, but I'm a heterosexual. No thanks. Just fucking with you!!!

My last two were the toughest. Went with Bowie's Modern Love—something from college. I was missing a genre, and that genre was southern rock. Easy choice. Lynyrd Skynrd, One More From The Road. I am as free as a bird now, and that bird will never change.

I called Dr. Steve and we made a deal. He wrote me two full pads of scripts, mostly different flavors of painkillers and nausea meds, left the date blank, and signed every page. I asked him for extra valium. Man, I do love a good valium. He told me if I made it long enough to run out, I could call his office and he'd mail me another two pads wherever I was at. Dr. Steve's the shit. Real fucking deal that one. I stopped by his office to pick them up, and filled my first few scripts at Walgreens.

I don't expect to call Dr. Steve, but I do expect to have a damn good time. Keeping those in the satchel with my trusty flask full of Jack Daniels to wash down the pills. Weird part is, I get past this hangover and I really don't have much pain.

THE LAST LETTER

Not sure I will. At this point, I'm putting on a blindfold and walking straight into Who The Fuck Knowsville.

I'm going to stop one last time at Wendell's, my favorite diner in Chicago and home of the hangover-curing greasiest biscuits and gravy in the city. It's off west Randolph, in case you ever get to town. Definitely for locals, so if you go, tell Wendell I said "hi".

I only have two things I want to do before the big day, D-Day. The day of my death. Swim one last time in the cold, rolling tide of the Pacific and get back to Yosemite for a few last climbs. I plan to head west on Interstate 90 as far as I can get. Thought about cuttin' across I-80 instead, but I'm skipping Iowa. Too much past to give the future it's due. I'm not doing this to recall memories. I plan to make them, even knowing they'll have a damn short shelf life.

Time to sign off, get this in the mailbox, and hit the road. Give my regards to Debbie and the kids.

Just Me,
Tracy

I read the letter four times as I finished my Camel. Each time, I painted a picture in my mind of the party, the packing, and the departure. The first letter was certainly more comforting than the last letter; definitely less shocking, and what I had expected from my friend. I put the letter back and covered the rest of the material. It was a solid first effort and easier than I had thought. I left the shop feeling less intimidated and more relaxed than relieved.

CHAPTER 7

THE LONG AND WINDING WESTERLY ROAD

Tracy's next letter was postmarked Sparta, Wisconsin. It was a short two-page note:

THE LAST LETTER

Dear Larry,

Fuck! Fuck! Fuck! Fuckitty fuck fuck! Dude, I'm lucky to be alive.

I got a late start out of Chicago. It was tougher to leave than I thought. I drove around a few old haunts one last time before hitting 90/94 north and west. I figured I had nothing to lose so I'd drive all night and get as far as I could into Minnesota before pulling off.

Around 7 I'm screaming around 80 m.p.h. about half an hour after dark. A fucking deer jumped out onto the interstate and a semi about 30-40 yards in front of me fucking demolishes it. It flew up and over and the back quarter dropped in front of me. Not braking for Bambi, I slammed into the carcass and dropped my bike. I was spinning like a top-down the interstate as sparks were shooting up from my leg guards like I was welding the right lane of the interstate.

I came to a stop just off the right shoulder and cars were slowing down to check on me. Good people in Wisconsin. My bike was in better shape than me. My leg guard is real fucked, but did save my ass. Still works. My back right trunk has a flesh wound, but nothing duct tape won't fix. All in all, not bad. I was fucking rattled though. I could still ride, but it shook the shit out of me.

Seems obvious God's going to kill me one way or another, but a deer? Really? A fu-cking deer???? No decent-minded god would let a dying man end it at the hands of a dismembered doe. Give me cancer—I get it. Kill me with a deer-fuck you!

A state trooper showed up and checked me and the bike out. Both were still legal and ready to ride, although he did tell me in his cheese-head accent that the deer are running this time of year and the road is no place to be at night on a motorcycle. Check that, Boss Hogg, no riding after dark.

I rolled three miles into the non-descript little town of Sparta and stopped at the first cheap hotel I could find. The clerk—a Mr. Rodgers looking guy, if Mr. Rodgers had a huge beer gut—looked at me and said, "Ahh, you da fella that played chicken with dat deer?" Guess news travels fast in the bumblyfuck woods of Wisconsin. "Der running this time of year ya know. Shouldn't be riding that thing after dark." Thanks, Melvin.

I grabbed my shit, threw it in my room, and went to the satchel—my mobile medicine cabinet. 2 valiums and a few long gulps of JD, and I was feeling better in about 5 minutes, and passed out cold in six.

I'm hungry as hell this morning. I dodged a god bullet. Time to eat and get the hell out of here. Next stop will be somewhere well before dark.

Give my regards to Debbie and the kids. Hug them tight and don't ride at night.

Just Me,
The Deerslayer

The letter was short enough, and I had half a Camel I had no intention of wasting, so I pressed on to the next three or four letters. Most were musings of the people he met in Minnesota and South Dakota and several detailed descriptions of encounters of various levels of interest. With my cigarette nearly out, I opened a letter from Rapid City, South Dakota with several pages front and back that while tempted, I knew I would never have time to read and stay within my hour allotment, and my timer was reminding me I was getting inconveniently close. I saved that for my next trip to the shop.

To Get To The End, Stop At The Start

I had always assumed that Tracy was born and raised in Arizona since he never spoke of any other place. That was not the case. I knew the letter would be a long read—it barely fit into the envelope. I unveiled the tarp and immediately pulled the letter out as soon as I got in the shop. It must have been the anticipation, but I did not light up a Camel. There was something in this letter and I had no time to waste to find out what it was given the hour I had available.

The letter was postmarked four days after the previous one. I was curious about the gap and, after reading the contents I fully understood the pause.

Dear Larry,

I'm finally checking out of Rapid City. It wasn't on my to-do list, but this is where it all started. I was born here and lived on 317 East Main until I was around four. My family lived in several places, and this was my starting point. It was the first of many houses we would live in until I finally settled at Grandma Bea's. The house on Main was similar to many we lived in—four total in the Phoenix area—small, with a major need for a fresh coat of paint.

We never stayed in any house for more than a couple years. People usually move because they either want to move FROM a place to escape a history that haunts them, versus moving TO a place because of a new opportunity—a job promotion, or the optimism of a new relationship. The newness always wears off by definition—something can't be new every day. My mom has moved every six to 18 months since I was in high school—always a place that will provide her a fresh start until the demons of her past catch up with her and force her to move again to the new fresh start.

I noticed in Pleasantville that there are people that move back, as we did with my mom, for the safety and security their past can provide. Or, simply because it's an easy place to be obscure if you're not originally from town—a place where you can't be found. And, there are some people, like you and Debbie, that never move because you don't expect a place to be new, you just have a life that never gets old, regardless of your street address. I've always respected that.

My dad always explained the Phoenix moves saying it was because he was transferred a lot for his job as an insurance adjuster. By the time I was old enough to realize that you don't move four times in 8 years in the same metro area because you got transferred it was too late to ask. I assume my parents moved hoping for a new start in each home, and that it never materialized. I didn't have the luxury of building any history in any one place until I got to Pleasantville, so my memories of Rapid City are pretty sparse.

One day while visiting my dad and stepmom in Texas I was rummaging through his closet—he is a world-class packrat. Keeps everything. In a Tupperware container, there was a green cardboard box filled with letters. They were letters he kept to and from my mom when we lived in Rapid City, all before I was born. A few were from Grandma Bea. I couldn't understand why they'd need to write letters if they lived together. Well, turns out my mom had a breakdown and spent several months in a mental hospital a few hours away in Mitchell before I was born. The letters reflected every bit of that. Reading them was surreal. I've never really understood mental illness and, really only came to better understand my mom's unique nature while I was in college. Those letters painted a vivid picture I never wanted to see and wished I hadn't. I never said a word to anyone about the letters. Ever. Most family secrets are better left untold.

Long and short of it is one day my mom was driving in a car with Tom and Katie, who had to have been around four and 2, and purposely tried to drive off the road to kill them all. It was in one of the letters. The story we were always told was that it was a snowstorm and she slid into a telephone pole. Nope. She was committed to a mental hospital after that and played the game well enough to finally get out. I'm not a psychiatrist, but if their job is to talk to people about the things I read in those letters, they don't get paid enough.

Funny thing is, I was born about five months after she was released. Either Mary and Ron had a brief conjugal visit somewhere in the asylum—certainly a possibility—or they didn't, which was the more likely explanation. There was nothing mentioned about her pregnancy in the letters and after I back-tracked the math I wondered for the first time if my dad was my biological dad. Didn't matter. I don't care about nature versus nurture. He's always been my dad, and a damn fine one, so the curiosity started and stopped after I closed the container and put it back in its place in the closet.

I've looked through enough photo albums to believe I was a happy kid, and Rapid City was a happy time. If pictures are worth a thousand words, not all thousand of them are true. There were plenty of smiles among us, but I assume there were more frowns that were never caught by the camera. Once we moved to Arizona when I was four the pictures told the same simple story of a lower-middle-class American family with high-gloss in the pictures and a much more pixilated reality.

My parents were divorced a couple years before we left Arizona for Iowa. They had been married 13 years. My mom's side of the story was that my dad's drinking was the cause, but even young kids know better. My dad liked to drink, but I rarely remember him drinking to excess. And, based on the letters from Rapid City, I wouldn't have blamed him if he did.

Mom got us kids and dad got an apartment after selling our house on Cypress Street. We moved in with my mom to a house in Paradise Valley in what I'd politely call a lesbian commune with ample narcotics around. My mom was the property of Jackie Briggs, to this day the meanest dike I've ever met. She had three kids and they were about our ages—Cindy, Scott, and Rick. There were two other single lesbians—Dion and Catherine, or "Cat", and several that would come and go with names not worth remembering. It was daily dysfunction and not a "trip down memory lane" any sane person would ever want to take.

My dad would get us on weekends and try to normalize the shitshow we lived during the week. It was pretty bad. No, it was very bad. Katie and Tom were old enough to keep it with them and I was just young enough to only have carry-on baggage. It was baggage none of us would take to Iowa or, until now, anywhere else. Drugs and mean lesbians create memories that are better left forgotten.

We ended up going to Iowa in a hell of a rush. My mom wanted out of the hippy-house and my dad was to take us to the airport. My grandparents paid for the plane tickets and agreed to let us live with them until we could better settle on our own. We were told to pack a single suitcase and that we weren't coming back. It didn't make sense when I was eight years old, and over twenty years later it still doesn't. I guess things like that aren't supposed to make sense.

My dad loaded the four of us in his car just when Jackie Briggs pulled into the driveway. After a good deal of yelling from the adults and screaming from the kids, she pulled a gun from her car and we took off. She followed us through red lights and heavy traffic all the way to the airport when my dad finally unloaded us and walked back to her car. I was sure he'd be shot. There was a lot of hand gesturing and yelling as we scurried into the airport terminal where dad finally met us to make sure we got on the Western Airlines jet safely.

Hours later we landed in Des Moines and my grandparents picked us up and took us home to Pleasantville. I have never told anyone how or why we ended up in Pleasantville, and I'd appreciate it if you do the same. Not even Debbie. I had always thought enough time would pass that I could tell this like any other story, but it's not any other story and I'm out of time to let it fade to the point where I'd want to recall it. I'm glad I can share it with you.

Katie, Tom, and I have only talked about it once, late one night we were all drinking together—which was very rare-- after Katie graduated from college. We each had such vivid memories of that morning so we helped each other fill in the blanks. Together we added depth and detail to a picture of a time we wished we could all forget.

I'm nearly done with my first roll of film. Good pictures. I'll send them to you when I get them developed down the road.

I've spent the last four days in Rapid City and the Black

Hills to see what came back to me, and what didn't. Or maybe shouldn't. Would have been a good place to raise kids. Good people. I'm glad I came here, where it—where I—started. I was able to rock climb a few times around Custer. I still have my climbing juju, and I hope that's the last thing to go. There is nothing that a couple of hours on a good solid granite face can't fix. Not even all of that. Good to bring it back, get it out of the way, and move on without it.

Give my regards to Debbie and the kids. You've been a great parent, and the world needs more like you. Both of you.

Just Me,
Tracy

After my third read, I shut off my timer and immediately lit a Camel, taking the first, deep hit like it would be my last. This would take more than my allotted hour. I stared at the folded papers and randomly around my shop. My mind went blank. I could not conjure a single thought, only a series of images-- each running through time like trying to connect pieces of a puzzle I thought I had already solved. I finally stepped back into the moment when my cigarette had burned down so far it singed my finger and thumb.

I put the letter back in the envelope and rather than set it back in its chronological space, decided to open the safe so it could take its place with my college writings and rarely—if ever—be read again, and certainly by no one but me.

I covered the pile, wiped some grease on my hands to cover the evidence of my Camel, as I had learned to do, and returned to the house to wash up. I was quiet at dinner, too quiet. Debbie asked what I was working on and all I could say was that it was a complicated project that would be hard to explain and that I was having a hard time getting it out of my head. "Must be a tough one.", was all she said. It was, indeed.

I did not go back into the shop for several days. I had to process what I read and what, very vividly in my mind, I saw and could not stop seeing. I had trepidation returning to read what the next letters may have in store. I did not know much about such things, but I wondered if after a four-day self-discovery and disclosure there may be a gap or pause. Possibly a new and deeper direction based on the images he saw in the reflecting pool he swam and nearly drowned in during his time in Rapid City.

I think when a person gets that deep in the pool of reflection and finally makes it back to shore, they either catch their breath and move on or languish in the exhaustion of simply surviving. If I was tired thinking about it, he had to have been exhausted to have gone through it.

I wasn't ready to see what was next while I was stuck on what just passed as if I were listening to a well-written song on a cassette tape then rewinding it over and over to find different meanings from the same lyrics. I would start in again when the replays in my mind stopped and I had settled in on a singular meaning for the lyrics and their relationship to the lyricist.

After an unusually mundane day at work and with a modest impatience for the standard dialogue of the patrons of the Rose City Café, I was ready for an hour in the shop to escape and start living my dead friend's life again. It was well into winter, so I turned the heater on, pulled open the top right drawer to light a Camel, took two short starter drags, and dove back into the next letters in the pile.

CHAPTER 8

THE RETURN OF MAYHEM AND MISCHIEF

The next parcel in the order was a large cardboard postal envelope, the first of many in the pile. It was postmarked from Rapid City and contained a Walmart photo envelope with forty-eight photos and no negatives. There were random shots of people, landscapes, a few gas stations, and a half dozen detailing the scrapes and scars on his motorcycle.

I had thought about trying to match the photos to where they may have been taken on my wall map but did not have the time or inclination to put those pieces of this puzzle together. That would wait for another day. I was ready to read what was next and had an hour to do it.

The next package was postmarked from Rozet, Wyoming. Inside was a small cassette tape. I had expected the tapes after the first letter, so I went to the Radio Shack in Knoxville early in the process and bought a mini-cassette player. I transcribed what I could from the ten minutes or so of tape. Those ten minutes took nearly my entire hour to accurately transfer to paper.

Reading is far easier than listening, but it was the first time I'd heard Tracy's voice in a few years. His voice wasn't the voice of a dying man. It was very much the Tracy I remembered, with a quick cadence and distinct pauses of thought, as though he was invisibly inserting commas and semi-colons into his verbal discourse. It was much more meaningful and comforting than reading words in cursive on paper. The contents, while not verbatim, were roughly as follows:

Dear Larry,

After Rapid, I decided on a change of course. Really more of a change in strategy. I was trying to get to my first goal of the Pacific as quickly as possible to check that off my list. I realized that last night in Rapid that I was driving by most of what I really wanted to see. I still hope to get to the ocean—and to Yosemite--but I need more depth than a cheap hotel room every night and a long, straight highway each day can provide.

I stopped in Newcastle, Wyoming for gas and bought a map—my first of the trip. I'd hope to live free and die free with no maps, no course, just driving to where the sun sets and hoping to wake up the next day. Honestly, the main reason I bought the map was that this neck of the woods is desolate as fuck and I wasn't about to die because I ran out of gas on a dustyfuck road in the middle of no man's land. The only benefit to that would be my body probably wouldn't be found for a few decades. My goal for the day was to get to Devil's Tower. Never been there and wanted to see what would have possessed Steven Spielberg to make it the focal point of Close Encounters of the Third Kind, and make Richard Dreyfuss sculpt it in his living room. Must be something to it.

Turns out, there really isn't. Dreyfuss should have left the clay with the kids. It's something cool surrounded by miles of what's not. Thanks to my map, I was able to take every type of road available to get there. Anything with a line on the map that would get me north and west. There's a whole lotta a nothing here. Words and pictures can't accurately assess it.

Screaming down the dusty roads did make me wonder who the fuck would live here and why. I also hadn't had a drop of alcohol since I got to Rapid City. Never had a desire while I was there, not even a quick sip of JD from my flask. What I had to do there had to be done sober. And, now that it is done, so too can my sobriety end.

By Newcastle, I was getting my thirst back, not just for a cold beer but for a friendly face to pour it. Plus, I was ready to get out of the mountains to the warmer temps of lower altitude. It's almost May and time to move from cheap motels into the wild to sleep under the stars. Wyoming seems like the best place to do it. Even bears are probably smarter than to live here, so it has to be safe. This place is why coyotes howl.

After my couple hour tour of the tower, I wound down to Carlile Junction—a spit off highway 14 that looked to have plenty of hidden places outside of town to settle for the night and the one thing I knew I'd find far more interesting than a tower the devil built—a narrow, long wood shack of a tavern across the street from a grain co-op and a stone's throw from the rusted railroad tracks that ran through the junction. There were two cars in the junction when I rolled in around four, but I figured with what was probably the only watering hole for miles it would fill up after dark. I set up a small camp under a large cottonwood tree next to a stream about two miles from town then took a dip in the stream to freshen up and slept a couple hours until dark.

I'm like Payden in Silverado, Larry. I do love a saloon. Or, tavern, club, or bar. It's my element. Wasn't always that way. In college, and even in Chicago those first couple years, going to a bar was an opportunity to accomplish two objectives that were better achieved with alcohol—getting laid, getting in a brawl, or--if I was lucky--both.

That was before I met Rex Chapman. Rex was my mentor at the agency. He rescued me from the copy room and taught me an ounce about advertising and ton about life. Rex was around 40 and was happily married with kids, until those times that he wasn't. That's usually when we went to a bar or club so he could remember who he was before soccer games, backyard barbeques with other yuppies complaining about their careers, and god-awful "date nights". We went out often with clients, co-workers, or just the two of us crafting our trade.

I'd traveled extensively with Rex for client pitches and he taught me the common nuances of every purveyor of alcohol. Always order a first drink for observation. What and who to look at and for. How to measure up the crowd and every person in it, what the vibe was and how to decide what our place would be within it.

Whether it was Paris, France, or Paris, Texas, we'd go into a bar and he'd point out subtleties I'd never noticed before. Who was talking to who and what they were talking about. The motives, some clear and some less, of each person and group. The dynamic. The flow. He could read people from across a table or across the room with the insight of Helen Keller with a book of braille. He was a personality savant.

And, the music. The music in any establishment is more important than the libations. What type and how loud? Who is dancing and who is watching? The music is the backdrop to everything that will or won't happen on a particular night. His observations were like fishing with a guide versus dropping a line and hoping for a bite. Take in every detail of the environment, pick your lure, then engage. But always do nothing but observe during that first drink. Always.

It was honestly the difference between walking into a grocery for a couple things you knew you needed and making a beeline to the check-out, versus strolling through an open-air market with an open mind and appetite with your senses stimulated, taking what tempted you at the time. Fucking life-changing.

In return for my evening education, my value to Rex was made very clear early on—I was the draw. I was young, athletic, good looking and had no fear or good sense. My job was to lure as many women to us as early in the night as possible so he could take over with his Jedi mind tricks. I'd hook 'em and he'd clean 'em and fry 'em. It worked very well with one catch. There's always a catch.

Rex would get first choice and I'd have to settle from

whoever was left. It was always unspoken, and I could usually tell within the first thirty seconds who his conquest would be and how he would do the conquering. Wasn't a big deal most of the time because we had different tastes. He opted for the woman that—like him—wanted no entanglement after the next morning, usually a fellow married sophisticate. I, on the other hand, wanted someone I could fall in love with for a few hours and get a phone number when we were done in case I wanted to fall in love with them for a few hours down the road. The few times we had our eyes on the same woman, I had to relent. The apprentice never gets to be the master.

Around seven I rode back into Carlile Junction, replaced my helmet with my trusty Old Style cap, and walked across a creaky wooden porch to the front door of the tavern, the Keyhole Tap. This place had been here since John Wayne was herding cattle up to Belle Fourche in The Cowboys. As I expected, there were about twenty vehicles parked out front—all pick-up trucks. I had a good feeling about it.

I opened the worn wooden door and walked inside. Hank Williams was playing. About six guys were around the pool table in the front room, each with a full pitcher of beer in front of them and not a single smile among them. They all had well-worn cowboy boots and self-shaped cowboy hats along with different patterns of flannel shirts that looked like they were bought several years ago and hadn't been laundered or pressed since.

The bar was dimly lit with a few neon beer signs scattered around and a back room that seemed better lit with a few long tables--must have been the banquet hall. I was the only person in hiking boots and baseball cap. Thank God I had a flannel shirt on over my t-shirt. If they would have seen it was a trusty

Patagonia, a city flannel, I'd surely have been in for a rather immediate ass-kickin'.

I ordered a Pabst Blue Ribbon draw. Not because I like PBR, mind you, but because it was the only beer they served. A straight PBR crowd meant they only had one taste and it wasn't very good. The big question would be if that taste included enjoying their beer with a stranger in the house. In bars like this, folks come in to get drunk, play pool and have a conversation or two. They're good people who've known each other well enough and long enough to keep the chit-chat to a minimum. They have no need for good company if it doesn't come from the company they're keeping.

While I was drinking that first beer taking it all in a few more people rolled in, including three women that all looked rode hard and put away wet. If one of my desires was companionship for the night, I'd have to drink a good deal more to accommodate it. I'd need more than beer goggles. I'd need a beer welding helmet.

Wasn't long into my second beer that the glances around the pool table turned into stares and ear whispers. I was a stranger in town, so I expected that.

When I asked the barmaid, Kendall—a tough-hided heavy woman probably around 50—for my second beer, she obliged. When she brought it back, she asked what brought me to town. "Just passin' through and stopping for a few." She asked where I was staying and I said, "Just down the road a ways." That seemed to satisfy her curiosity. I wasn't going to rob the place, and probably wasn't a serial killer, so she had all the information she needed from me in order to walk off and tend to the regulars.

When you're a stranger in a locals' bar you have to mind

your own and be ready for the inevitable challenge. Most places like this don't mind out of towners, but they definitely don't like strangers. If you're different, you best finish your first beer and be on your way. Everybody's thirsty, but not everybody is welcome.

Younger men, like those around the pool table, are like wolves. They travel in packs and piss in the corners to mark their territory. At some point between the first beer and after the last, they'll normally send a scout to investigate a stranger to decide whether and how to attack, whether to keep their distance, or whether to let the rogue pass through without hassle. I'd been through the chess match plenty of times in plenty of places and had plenty of ways to deal with it.

First, always pick a seat at the middle of the bar. Don't let yourself get cornered and don't look like a loner who's here to steal their cattle or kick their dog. Look like you're willing to have someone sit on either side. It's the friendliest seat at the bar, least threatening. The center also gives you the best vantage point to the bartender, and it's always the bartender that will help guide the pack on how an outsider gets treated.

You want to talk up the bartender early and choose your words carefully. Ask their name, do they own the bar, how long they've been bartending. Tell them it seems like a nice place, then stop right there. Too many questions and you'll stop getting answers and instead get a cold, quick invite out of the tap. They want to know your business more than you ought to know theirs.

When the scout comes, and they always do, they'll always start with a simple interrogation. The questions they ask and the way they ask them will tell you their intent, like a bad poker player trying to find out how strong your hand is. Your tell is how you respond. And how you respond has a quick and direct correlation on how long and how well your evening will last.

This night at the Keyhole Tap the scout wandered over from the pool table and put a dead pitcher on the bar right next to me for Kendall to fill. He was a stocky guy, about my height, with a fat dip in his front lip and his worn white straw cowboy hat covering a tight crewcut. He leaned on the bar waiting for service, stared at me, and asked if I was new to town, knowing damn well I wasn't. In places like this, they know you're new before you get there. "Just passin' through," I said looking him dead in the eye. That's a polite way of saying, "Leave me the fuck alone."

"Where ya headin'?"

"Got some business further west."

"Whereabouts?"

At "whereabouts" the pace of the interrogation picked up enough that I could see this one was heading south. I redirected—a great strategy--and asked, "I didn't catch your name."

"Roy".

Of course it was fucking "Roy". This is the middle of bumfuck Wyoming. I looked over my shoulder at the rest of the pack, cues in hand, staring at me and Roy, and thought, "There's Cooter. And, Skinny Jim. And Tiny—usually the fattest of the bunch. Nobody named Tiny is really tiny. And, there's got to be a Tex in there, even though he's probably not from Texas." The rest were likely some variations of a Chuck, a Billy or a Big Joe—there's usually a Big Joe—a big guy that's probably mildly retarded. In bars like this, you'll never find a Brad, a Keaton, or Sean like a good city bar. The faces are different, but the names and personalities are always the same in a place like this.

"How about you, stranger?" Well, this was a dilemma. A damn dilemma. "Tracy" would have made the work of any brawl a lot harder and likely more painful. "Scott" wasn't going to do me much better. Lawyers are named "Scott". How and why I still don't know, but I calmly blurted out, "Buck". "Buck" says I've been in this spot before and I'm ready if I need to be, and that I'm strong enough that any attack will come at a cost. Buck is always somebody's best friend. A natural leader. No one has ever not liked a "Buck". I finished, "Buck McGuire".

Kendall came back with Roy's pitcher and he threw a five on the bar, then pulled out another single and said, "Get the fuckin' Irishman a round, too." Scrappy-Do walked back to the pack to report his findings while I looked at Kendall and said, "I'm not here lookin' for trouble. Just havin' a few beers." She leaned both forearms on the bar and said, "Those boys get enough beer in 'em and you'll find plenty of trouble. I'd finish this one and be on my way if I were you." My problem was that "on my way" was two miles outside of town under a cottonwood tree, which is a premier place to follow a stranger and kick the shit out of them.

After about an hour I was pulling out my wallet to order another draw and the biggest one of the group—definitely the alpha male—walked up to the bar with nothing but his pool cue in hand, stood to my left, and said, "Mister Buck, I think you've had enough to drink tonight." I'd had four beers and a thirst for several more. I looked him in the eye respectfully and asked, "What's your name?".

"Rusty.", he said.

Fuck, a "Rusty". I forgot all about a Rusty. Goddammit!

Rustys and Dustys are usually the chief enforcers in a crew like this—bigger, meaner wild cards that will always give or take the first hit. They're nearly as bad as a "Butch". Butches are the worst. A Butch will eat your kidneys after kicking your ass. I won't often tangle with a Butch, and avoid any chance they'll want to tangle with me.

There were several options I was considering at that point, and only had a few seconds to choose. I didn't think they were drunk enough yet to want a full-on brawl, but it was early in the night so I wasn't ready to head out the door to get my ass-kicked sleeping under a tree by a half dozen drunken cowboys. The only option was to piss in my corner--mark my territory--and see what happened next. Ballsy move, but the only move that made sense at that very moment.

I stood up. Rusty was about three inches taller than me. Around 6'2". I looked straight into his eyes and as slowly, calmly, and confidently as I could, said, "Rusty, I'm going to stay and have a few more beers, maybe even talk to the ladies over there a bit. So, if you motherfuckers want a piece of me you better take a bite right fucking now while I'm still feelin' civil. Doesn't matter to me either way." We looked at each other for about five seconds while the rest of bar stared at the exchange. It was a game of chicken, as they all are, and the secret is to never flinch first.

Rusty managed a cautious grin and a low nod. The flinch. He then in a slightly welcome tone told me if I was going to talk to the girls I oughta meet the boys first. The pack was letting the rogue mosey through. Four hours later: Crisis avoided. Friends made. Pool played. And pitchers consumed. A damn fine night all the way around.

After the bar closed we went to Kris's house about half a

mile from the junction—I never would have guessed there'd be a Kris in the group, especially a Kris with a "K"—had a few more beers and cooked some bacon and eggs. I got back under the cottonwood tree around two in the morning and had the best night of sleep since I left Chicago.

Listening to the tape was the first time I'd laughed through the process. It was reminiscent of the Tracy I knew. I'd been a spectator in that very scene several times with several different outcomes so it felt like I was leaning against the far wall of the bar watching a movie I'd seen many times before, never with the same ending. It was like I WAS there because I had BEEN there.

My hour was up, my Camel long expired. It was time to head back to the house.

The next several envelopes and a few packages detailed much of the same—a meandering path to a tiny tavern in the middle of nowhere to meet new people and let them meet him, making more friends than enemies, and leaving no trace upon his departure. There were a few conquests and several nights spent under the stars, including a night sleeping at the "Hole In The Wall", Butch Cassidy's hideout, that came with a long dissertation on the Sundance Kid. If I wasn't well into the stack of envelopes with more to go, I would have thought this is how and where it all would have ended and it would have been a fine and fitting end at that.

On my next trip to the shop, with Camel in hand, I opened the next parcel in line, which meant it was another tape. It was postmarked from Rock Springs, Wyoming. It was as quick as it was hilarious with Tracy talking in a hushed and rushed tone:

LARRY REYNOLDS

Dear Larry,

I don't have much time to get this to the post office, so I'll try to be quick. I'm putting an end to what was probably the best day of this—well, let's call it a trip--and one of the better days of my life. I just spent the last few hours in jail and the Sweetwater County courthouse where my Wyoming privileges have now been officially revoked. Too bad because I've had a hell of a good couple of weeks here. Good people in general and a low shitbird ratio.

According to the Sweetwater County magistrate, the Honorable Mike McCallister, "I know every sheriff in the 23 counties of Wyoming. If any of them find you in this state after today they'll bring you to me to rot as long as it takes in the county jail." I need to gas up and get the hell to Utah or Idaho before dark. Probably Idaho. Not sure there are any bars in Mormon country.

The day actually started pretty shitty. I've been having some pain and a few chills now and then, mostly at night, but nothing a few Percocet or valium and a Meclizine couldn't get me through. About five minutes after I woke up this morning, my stomach was in knots. Like there was a wrestling match going on inside. I crawled out of my sleeping bag on my hands and knees for about ten feet and puked till I cried. Literally fucking cried!

One of the symptoms Dr. Steve told me about was, "increasingly intense nausea". The nausea I had wasn't increasingly intense and it definitely wasn't from this world. The shit I puked up wasn't from a human. I was convinced I had one of those little fuckers from Aliens inside me and it was going to rip my stomach open to get out. Goddamn it! Where was Ripley when I needed her? I took a half handful of meds and washed them down with a quart of water, packed up, and was on my way.

I blew through a stop sign at Farson getting on highway 119. Didn't see the cop. How can you not see a fucking cop in place where you can see everything for 200 fucking miles? He turned on the cherries and pulled me over. Just as he was getting out of his car, I realized I hadn't had a high-speed chase on my list of things to do when I die; that I should; and that this was my best chance to check that box. I peeled out and took off. The faster I went, the funner it got. I just kept thinking, this is exactly how I ought to die...fuck them! Yes, Maverick and Goose, I had a need. A need for speed.

I got off the pavement onto dirt roads. Top speed was 112, which is fast as fuck on a dirt road. Goldwings are made for 112, but they're not made for 112 on gravel. It was like I'd kicked the scrotum of a wild bull. I was riding a Clydesdale in a damn steeplechase, but today the Clydesdale was hungry—and pissed off!

Within 15 minutes I could see four cop cars in my rear view mirror chasing me across timber roads and dusty trails, each trying to converge on me from a different direction. Fuck yes! I got inspired by Butch and Sundance and figured if I could get off-road and into the mountains they'd never be able to follow me. I crossed cattle gates and rode fence lines for another 20 minutes, dropping the cars as I went. At one point I spun a few high-speed donuts on the other side of a dirt road, rode a hundred yards and turned around, and cranked the gas. I jumped the culvert through the dust and between two cop cars and spooked one of them into the ditch. Epic move. Fucking straight-up epic! Honestly, it spooked the fuck out of me, too, but I was having too much fun to notice.

I kept waiting for Bon Jovi's "Blaze of Glory" to ring through my ears, but all I heard was the high-pitched whining of those 1500 cc's, and the snap, crackle, and pop of my shocks as they no doubt were wondering what the fuck I was doing to them.

Jesus, it was fucking D.B. Cooper legendary! Goldwings aren't made for off-road, but today mine was. That thing's a fucking stallion—a quarter ton fucking stallion! I was screaming through prairies, pastures, and woods until I finally crossed a cattle grate up a long, dusty lane that went straight to a big rock outcropping where I figured I'd ditch the last few cars for good. At the end of the long, dusty lane there was a small cabin and in the middle of the long, fucking dusty lane was an old guy on a horse with a shotgun pointed straight at me. Well, goddamit.

I dumped my bike trying to avoid the horse and the engine died. I got up and took my helmet off slowly, figuring I had time to talk the old-timer into letting me pass. He was having none of it. Told me to stand still or he'd shoot me on the spot. He said, "Sheriff radioed me and told me you might be happening by." What kind of sheriff radios a fucking citizen? What bored fucking citizen is on the other end of a radio? The great fucking citizens of Wyoming! Fuckers!

Within three minutes there were four cop cars around me and six deputies with different variations of firearms pointed at me. I didn't mind the thought of dying going off a cliff or busting through a barn, but I had no flavor for getting shot, and these were the type of boys that'd have no problem doing just that. City cops shoot to survive. Mountain cops shoot to kill, and I bet they're damn good at it. Death by the high-speed toxicity of a lead bullet is no way to die. Sorry, John Bon Jovi—this would not be my Blaze of Glory moment.

The sheriff, an older guy with a paunch, a finely pressed hat,

THE LAST LETTER

and a mustache that looked like a fucking bird's nest walked up to me with his pistol—a damn ivory-handled revolver, which was impressive--cocked and just said, "Mister, you're going to jail." I didn't even respond. As you recall from our big night out with Pete Spaulding pointing his rather mundane service revolver in my car, I knew the best thing was just to put my hands up and let the process play out.

The sheriff waved one of his deputies over and said, "Bill, get that bike back to county." Then the sheriff cuffed me and set me in the caged back seat of a tricked-out Ford Bronco. Took a half hour to get to Rock Springs and the only conversation was, "That's a mighty nice bike.", from the sheriff and "Thanks.", from me.

I was processed at county. Speeding. Resisting arrest. Threatening a law enforcement officer—that was bullshit. Trespassing. There were a few others and all in all, it seemed like a pretty accomplished list to me. They tossed me in a cell. They took all my shit but—thank god—didn't put me in one of those fucking orange jumpsuits. Nobody looks good in orange and you shouldn't wear a jumpsuit until you're at least 75. Still kept my cuffs on though. Pricks.

About four hours went by and a deputy took me from my cell to the judge. People in Wyoming don't talk much, but the real mutes must go into law enforcement. No small talk. Not a word. Just a walk down a long hall with light blue concrete walls and a nice polish on the linoleum floor.

Judge McCallister read the offenses and the jail time and fines associated— a total of $425 and six months in jail--and asked, "Son, just what the hell were you thinkin'?"

He told me they searched my bike and found drugs, but I had prescriptions, so I was fine there. A little whiskey, which is no-harm, no-foul in Wyoming. It's practically required. But no contraband and no weapons. My first break.

"Why didn't you just be a decent motorist and get your traffic ticket?"

I thought about going Al Pacino from "And Justice For All" and shouting, "You're out of order. This whole court is out of order!", but didn't seem that would get me too far.

I calmly told the judge that the prescriptions were for pain medications because I had terminal cancer and only a few months to live so I didn't have time to stop for a traffic ticket."

He said, "Mr. McGuire, I've heard enough lines of crap in the past 27 years to fill a honey wagon. But, I will say that's the first time I've ever heard that."

I told him he could call Dr. Steven Glasgow at Chicago Rush Hospital who would confirm it.

He responded, "He might have been stupid enough to let you go, but I'm not. You'll be remanded to custody for six months in county after you pay your fine. Can you pay your fine?"

I told him my money was in my satchel in the back trunk of my bike, and that I'd pay double if he'd drop the six months in county. He firmly said, "Absolutely not." I calmly explained that the good taxpayers of Sweetwater County wouldn't like the cost of taking care of a dying man—it's very expensive, and I doubt I'd make it the entire six months. He leaned back and folded his arms, then—after about a minute—shook his head and said, "Pay your fine at the clerk's desk. Better be cash. You'll be released on one condition.

Then, his Magistrate Mike speech: "I know every sheriff in the 23 counties of Wyoming and if any of them find you in this state after today they'll bring you to me to rot as long as it takes *in the county jail." Seemed like a good compromise, and a damn good time to put the Equality State in my rear view mirror.*

Took me about an hour to get my shit, pay my dues and get the hell out of there. I figured it wasn't right to leave such a good place after such a good compromise without celebrating with a quick, cold beer. There was a half-ass bar a block down from the county jail, so I pulled my bike up and stopped in.

Sure enough, the honorable Sheriff Lee Hartman with his bushy-ass mustache was sitting at the bar having a beer. I stepped up to the stool next to him and asked if he'd mind if I had one last beer before leaving his beautiful state.

"Long as it's just one.", he said, noting he was just off his shift.

I asked the bartender to pour a Budweiser—the King of Beers being the only thing on tap—and apologized to the sheriff for the trouble I caused.

He took a long drink and with the froth still shrouding that fucking shag carpet under his nose said, "Well, to be honest, that's one of the better times I've had the past 15 years as sheriff. You sure know how to handle a bike, especially a big one like that." He went on, "Was that a crock of shit you told the judge?".

"No, sir".

"Well, I'm sorry to hear that."

"I appreciate that, sheriff."

We sat for another five minutes and just looked at the TV on the wall—it was like Maury Povitch or some shit— and sipped our beer. I was about down to the bottom of the glass.

He looked and said, "Glad you're not going to die in Wyoming, but it wouldn't be the worst thing if you did."

I tapped his glass with mine and said, "It's a helluva place". I asked the bartender to pour another draw for the sheriff and settled up. It was a good way for Wyoming to end. Time to hit the road.

Give my regards to Debbie and the kids. Life is short, Larry. Drink every drop.

Just Me,
Tracy

CHAPTER 9

THE AGENCY

We often wondered about Tracy's job. When he would come home those first few years he was quick to point out that he worked at an ad agency in Chicago, Maxwell-Collins, or "MC Hammer-Can't Touch This", as he would refer to it. He did it to impress, but with close friends, he disclosed that like many of us he felt he was in a dead-end job that sucked the life out of him but paid his bills.

There was no glamour in his description to those of us close to him. However, a big city advertising job seemed to impress the elderly ladies of the bridge club in town, and his grandmother--a very modest woman--would beam when they would ask what he was doing after college. She seemed happy to pronounce that he was both a big city boy turning into a man and setting the advertising world on fire. Based on his accounts, neither seemed to be true.

His tape from the desert of southern Idaho told a very different story, and one that helped explain how his job afforded a life of travel and time-off which few of the rest of us could relate. It was a long recital and provided context into both a profession I will never know and the few breaks and the few people that, timed just right within a career, can spell the difference between a life of rags or riches.

Larry,

There's that old saying that when you die your tombstone will never read, "I wish I'd spent more time at the office." As I sit off a forest service road in a small stand of pines, I can tell you—I do miss my job, and I know it's one of the things I'll miss the most as I die.

When I graduated, I packed what I could in my Cutlass and drove to Chicago. I wanted to play rugby and I wanted to be able to say that I not only survived, but thrived in one of the best cities in the world. I crashed on Steve Gulick's

THE LAST LETTER

couch in the small apartment on Dearborn that he and his girlfriend--and eventual wife—shared. He was the only person from Central I knew in Chicago and the only free place to stay while I interviewed. And interviewed. And interviewed more. I interviewed for every opening in the Tribune. I'd put my cocoa brown prom suit and tie on every day and hit the streets. I was looking for any job that could pay the rent, and that's about all I got.

I started in the copy room at Maxwell-Collins, a mid-market ad agency with about 120 employees. Mid-market means they focused on smaller clients, leaving the big brands to BBDO, Saatchi and Saatchi, and Zenith. While we were mostly regional around the Great Lakes, we had clients around the country. The key selling point was they were the only company that offered me a job that wasn't in the grocery or fast food business. When you got nothing, you got nothing to lose.

My starting pay sucked--$19,500 a year—and so did my job. The copy room is literally right next to the mail room in the basement, and for good reason. This is the bottom of the ladder. Climbing the ladder out of the copy room is next to impossible. I worked with around 25 copywriters, some that had been there for years and others, like me, that were hired so they could wash out within a few months.

Every job has a pecking order, and an ad agency is no different. Even in the copy room, the top of the rung are the jingle writers—musical types that focus on radio and TV ads and generally think their shit doesn't stink. You know the "Roto-Rooter" tune you can't get out of your head? You can thank MC jingle writers Ben Thomas and Karen Heaberlin for that. When your kids tell you your bologna "has a first name, it's O-S-C-A-R...", that's Maxwell Collins at work.

Then there are the lesser types—like me—that worked on print ad copy, tag lines, and—if you were lucky—a TV commercial script. Each day I'd get brown inter-office envelopes with a string wrap, like some "Mission Impossible" assignments. The creative team would have a client and campaign fact sheet. Sometimes the art team would throw in a few images. The research team would have useless data. Then, you were given your specific task to create copy for.

Honestly, even at $19,500 a year, I was stealing from them. I couldn't write for shit those first several months and figured I'd be out of a job once they figured that out. I did have a few good tag lines to my credit, but nothing that would take me anywhere but out of the agency and back into the job hunt.

I was lucky in that the copy room supervisor, guy named George Trower, liked my enthusiasm and knew I was a grinder. Like any editor, he'd redline my work like Sandy Hildeman in 9th grade English. He'd crucify the other copy writers' work— even the jinglers. Most of us in the room hated him, and all of us feared him. He was a nerd—big, black rim glasses, pocket protector, the whole package. He'd been with the agency 20 years and knew his shit, and he didn't take it from any of us.

The magic finally happened when I got an assignment from the South Dakota Bureau of Tourism. They needed a print campaign for the area and had a few photos. I came up with the line, "More Rush! More Beauty! Visit Mount Rushmore and the Famous Black Hills!". I wrote a quick two-page insert on all the things to do in the Black Hills, and it stuck. The client loved it and I found my calling—I was the king of the travel insert.

Seriously, you give me a few pictures of Northwest Bumfuck Egypt and tell me if the ad is for tourism or business development and I'd write complete bullshit that would make you want to build your dream house there. Desert of Kazakhstan? You'll move your company there thanks to the great educational foundation, low labor costs, and business-friendly tax benefits… all complete crap.

I'd never been to most of the places I wrote about, but I'd go to the library and look up a few things in the Encyclopedia Britannica and make up the rest. It wasn't much of a gift, but it was the only gift I had. My stuff ended up in airplane magazines and travel brochures. Once in a while, I'd see it and it was a pretty bitchin' feeling.

I got a bump in pay and moved into my loft with nothing but a used recliner and a few garage sale dishes and glasses. No curtains. No pictures. Just a mattress and a recliner. All I really needed. My job sucked, but it was a means to an end—I really came to Chicago to play rugby for the Lions, so as long as I had a shower, a two-burner hot plate, and a sink, I was good to go.

After a couple years of putting my copy back in the folder so it could be couriered up to the client team that handled the account so they could shit all over it, I started going up the elevator to the third floor where the client managers were to hand-deliver it. Pissed the other copy writers off, but if you're going to kiss ass, you have to know the right asses to kiss and how big a smooch they'll need.

A client management team is also a hierarchy. There are usually two middle-aged women that gate-keep for the Client Manager. Work them just right—ask about their kids, joke with them about this and that, and generally be brief but charming, and you'll get the right eyes on your work. Then, there are the creative and research assistants—mostly young aggressive types, usually women, that do the majority of the work. The Client Manager is always a man. Advertising is a man's world, which I always thought was bullshit because the women usually have the best ideas and the worst pay, but I was blessed with testicles and it's a system I wouldn't be able to change, so I rolled with it.

If you're a Client Manager and woo enough clients for enough years, and have enough drinks at the club with old man Collins or Mr. Maxwell, you get moved up to the fourth floor—the top floor. Big offices, big money, and from what I could see not much to do. As my dad has told me, "Those jobs aren't hard, but they are hard to get."

It would have been a hell of a long swim for me to touch the edge of the 4th floor, so I did my best to parlay what I could with the seven Client Managers. Fortunately, one bit. My mentor, Rex Chapman. One day when I was dropping a copy project off with Sheila, one of his assistants, he came out and said, "Are you that farm boy that's making all the noise down in the copy room?". Everyone assumes if you're from Iowa you grew up on a farm. I rolled with it. He asked me to grab lunch with him and we both knew it wasn't lunch at all—it was an interview to plan my escape from the hell-hole of the copy room.

Rex started every lunch with a Manhattan and finished with an equally potent Rob Roy. In the middle, he'd eat a little and ask a lot of questions. Like a machine gun with his North Shore accent, he'd usually start the next question before I finished answering the first. Our first date went well and he asked me to have a few drinks after work a few days later. I was charming the charmer, until I wasn't. After about six beers, the Tracy in me came out and I got bold and stupid, like Pavlov's dog in a bar—I was conditioned to either get laid or get in a fight.

Rex said, "Jesus farm boy, you're not just rough around

the edges, you're rough all the way through." I thought I was fucked, but he asked me to stop in his office the next morning and required that I stay out of jail in the meantime. In his office he offered me a position with a very clear catch—I was there to listen and nod, but I was never to speak unless he invited it. I'd never heard of "Shut The Fuck Up" on a job description, and if it was, I'd never have been able to put it on my resume. I knew it was going to be tough to hold back a lifetime of talking, but there was money and freedom on the line, so—like The Dude--I had to abide.

He told me I would be his project. Said I'd likely fail but he wouldn't because he doesn't know how to fail. God, I loved the confidence of that mother-fucker. Then he gave me $700 in cash and walked me out of the agency to shop for clothes the rest of the morning. The cocoa brown suit from prom wasn't going to impress anyone. In fact, I'm not even sure it impressed my prom date, Rhonda.

We went to Hart Marx for a new wool suit and Brooks Brothers for shirts and ties. One last stop at Neiman Marcus for an expensive pair of shoes that I only used for clients—never day to day. Over the course of the next few years, Rex taught me everything. It was like reform school for the socially retarded. How to eat. When to laugh. How to read a room and how to channel your charm—too much is far worse in an ad pitch than too little.

I didn't learn much about advertising, but that wasn't what my education was about. I learned about business. About the schmooze—how to oil the machine. I learned it damn well. I was his protégé. He was the sculptor and I was the clay to be formed in his image. I still to this day owe him everything.

After a year or so, he started calling me "Fire McGuire"

in meetings and client pitches. It was never just "Fire". It was always "Fire McGuire," said in some sort of gravelly-voiced bold Chicago poetic rhythm like "Da-Bears". For a year or so I thought it was because I was full of fire—great ideas. Enthusiasm. Talent. Turns out, that wasn't the case.

A couple years after the Fire McGuire myth was getting traction, we had a long flight delay at the airport in Scranton after we bombed a client pitch—straight up fucking bombed it— and, naturally, spent the idle time in the bar. Rex had just enough bourbon to tell me the truth. He said, "Kid, you ever wonder why I call you Fire McGuire?"

"Because I'm full of fire? Like, great ideas and piss and vinegar and all that."

"You're so fucking simple. I love it.", he laughed as he was shaking his head. "No, Big Man, it's because those first couple years you'd fuck up so much in meetings that about once a month old man Maxwell would tell me, 'Fire McGuire!'. I liked the sound of it. Sort of rolls off the tongue." Then he looked at me as serious as six bourbons can let you be and said, "Fact is, Kid, I've fought for you and I'm glad I did. Now that Tom's gone, you're going to be my next Assistant Client Manager."

Client managers make big money, Larry, and as a junior, I would be doubling my salary with a hell of a bonus if we did well—and Rex always did well. He didn't know how not to do well. I'd be next in line for Rex's job when he eventually gets promoted. Not really sure if that would have been the case, and not because I had to leave to go die. It didn't matter.

I'd started to notice in meetings that while the rest of the pitch team used their skills to present research, story boards, and budgets, Rex usually used me just to relate to the client. If it was a room full of dudes, he'd pause at breaks and say,

THE LAST LETTER

"Fire McGuire, tell the boys here about climbing Kilimanjaro. That blizzard story is one of my favorites." Or, "Fire McGuire, tell the guys here about life on the farm.". If there were women in the room, he'd ask me to share a rugby recap from the previous weekend, or some fabrication of being raised by a single mom. Anything that could connect me—and the agency—to the client. He would always prompt me with the context and knew just which stories he wanted me to tell.

I then realized that I was nothing but a show pony. He didn't need my insight. I didn't have a ton of creative ideas. I couldn't walk my way through a budget if my life depended on it. Market research bored the hell out of me. No, he needed me for my stories, and he taught me when and how to tell them. My more-skilled teammates were noticeably jealous of me. I lacked their substance and they lacked my paycheck. I'd have been pissed off, too.

The benefit to me, besides the money, was that Rex needed more content. More stories. So, when I'd tell him I needed a couple weeks off to climb in Antarctica, he'd gladly oblige. A four-day tournament in California? "Go get 'em, Tiger." Hell, I'd take around eight to ten weeks of vacation a year following my passions and it was not just allowed but encouraged by Rex because Maxwell-Collins needed the stories. And, so did Rex. I was his lure and whether we were in a board room or a nightclub, he'd dangle that lure to draw interest that he would ultimately use to close the deal. And, we closed a lot of deals in both board rooms and bars.

The toughest part of taking this journey wasn't keeping my situation from my family. It wasn't quitting the Lions—I'd never be able to compete in rugby at that level again. It was telling Rex I was leaving and lying to him about why. I couldn't use the "job in another country" story that worked well for everyone else that I told. He'd have offered to raise my pay. I couldn't tell him I was sick. Just couldn't. I sat across from him in his office and I told him my dad had cancer so I had to leave to take care of him. I asked if I'd be welcome to come back to the agency when my business was done with my family.

He poured us each a small glass of damn good scotch that, up until that point, I'd never had access to. He leaned across his desk, tapped my glass, and raised a toast. "You're a better man than I expected, Fire, and you never learned that from me. Go do the right thing."

We finished our scotch like fine men do, shook hands and I walked out of the agency doors for the last time. I made it about two blocks and stepped into an ally and cried. It was the only time during all this bullshit that I've cried. It didn't last long, and I'm not sure why it happened. I wish I could go back, but that's not how all this is supposed to work.

I'll close hoping you're doing well in your job and may someday miss it as much as I do mine. Give Debbie and the kids a hug for me. You're a great dad and a solid provider.

As Always,
Tracy

Tracy's professional progression matched very well with what we witnessed on his trips back home. He had become polished, much more so than any of us. Unlike many of our other collegiate classmates, his polish was simply a varnish. We all have different degrees of persona change in our professional and personal lives, but for many the tendency is to migrate to one at the expense of the other. Few can blend them well, and he had become one of those few.

When he would return home he aptly slipped back into the small-town kid from State Street that we'd all been accustomed to and was able to do so quickly and rather comfortably. With both personas, there was an added maturity provided as the years passed.

Tracy's personal and professional lives had become symbiotic, creating success for one based on a reliance on the other. Whether he showcased it in the streets and meeting rooms of the city or not, he seemed proud of his roots and it was a grounded pride. I was one of the few that noticed the nuance. He had not "gone city" on us as others had, and I have little doubt he played the country boy card in his job only when it would benefit him—and his agency--most.

I was happy to see that he had finally realized and harnessed one of his true gifts—his chameleon-like ability to adapt to whatever social setting he found himself in. A chameleon uses camouflage to avoid predators or draw in prey and both are necessary for survival. A composite of its surroundings, the disguise will never allow a revelation of its true identity or intent.

He had become an actor moving from stage to stage, comfortable in the part he was to play at any given time. He became aware of the stage and the expectations of the audience, which was something up to that point he had not been able to do. I'm sure his mentor, Rex Chapman, deserved much of the credit for the transformation. I also am of the strong belief that the value system of a small Midwestern town—the strong and subtle day-to-day development of life-long relationships--allowed him to transform more successfully.

More importantly, his mentorship had moved him from the grit and confinement of the arena into the broader view afforded by the stands. He had finally, it seemed, realized that he could learn lessons not solely from his own failures but from the successes enjoyed—and passed along to him—by others. It was subtle, yet it was powerfully transformational.

CHAPTER 10

WESTWARD HO AND THE HORTICULTURIST

A few letters from various towns in Idaho and Utah and a parcel with another roll of random photos from the Great Salt Lake were next. There were musings and modest ponderings of the day's activities, the people he met and the plans he was making, the starry nights and warm, dry, desert days.

Then, there was a poignant, reflective tape postmarked, "Winnemucca, Nevada". I only had enough time left in my hour to play it through one time:

Dear Larry,

I have traveled to nearly every part of the world. Six of the seven continents—missed Australia, damn it! I have always wondered where the armpit of the world is, and I wonder no more. I've just spent the past two days in Winnemucca, Nevada. After a damn long drive across the Great Salt Lake Desert—a hell of a forbidding place in its own right—I got into town just before dusk. Still not going to drive during the dark, by the way. There may not be much around here but I bet there are deer. If there are deer in Wisconsin, there must be some near Winnemucca.

Winnemucca is an ugly desert town at dusk and it never got any better in the light of the next day. This is where dreams go to die. It's about 5,000 people and even the kids have weathered faces and a mysterious look like they're wondering, "How the fuck did I get here?"

There are several casinos, and every bar, restaurant, and gas station has slots. I like a good casino. Actually, I love a good casino. I'd even manage with a piss on the floor casino. These casinos are worse, by both character and content. Needless to

THE LAST LETTER

say, Johnny Cash was right—if you've been to Winnemucca, you've been everywhere, man.

For the first time in a week, I was hungry. The nausea isn't consistent, but when it hits, it hits like thunder and takes a few hours to get anything down. I try to get as much in me as possible when I do get that golden, wonderful, incredible pang of hunger. Usually it's something as bad for me as possible— gas station hot dogs with extra pre-fabricated chili sauce are a frequent favorite. Throw some fucking Cheeze-Whiz on one of those fuckers and, well, it's better than probably 37% of the sex I've ever had. Bag of Doritos, even better. A full-on non-diet cola mixed in with a quart of buttermilk is a bonus. While I'm glad I treated my body like a temple with fucking wheat germ, oat groats, and a low-fat diet with protein shakes for dessert for all those years, it was time to die-hard and what I consumed was the best way to do it. Maybe I'll get lucky and have a heart attack before the cancer kills me…let the diseases fight for my ultimate demise. Fuckers.

I ended up staying at the beautiful Winnemucca Inn, the oldest casino in town. It looked like it. It smelled like it. Last renovation was likely before the stage coach. I thought it might have historical value, but based on the luxury of my room I imagine most of these rooms are rented by the hour. I didn't have to pay extra for clean sheets, so it was a fair deal at $49 a night. After checking in and getting the key with a belt-buckle-sized "Get Lucky 777" scarred brass key tag attached, I headed to the restaurant, figuring to fuel up before a good night at the tables.

I had my choice of the all-you-can-eat buffet for $3.99 or the "fine dining" of the aptly named "7-11" restaurant; aptly named because the food was akin to a convenience store with a *grill. After the greasiest steak and baked potato with layers of every product Kraft could conjure placed on top of it, I headed to the bar. It was an easy trip as it was the same place.*

I was having my first drink sizing up the place. Always, Larry, always. There were a few locals, most of which looked like gambling addicts that fell on hard hits from the dealer for enough years that they'd only come in the day their welfare check dropped in the mailbox. Also, a few truck drivers stopping for the night off I-80 to try their luck with the machines or the Mary Kay-laden women that wandered the parking lot looking for immediate income. And, poor dying bastards like me. If I have incurable cancer most of the people in this place look like they've had it a lot longer, and a lot harder, than me.

While the tables had a soft allure to me, the thought of either taking good money from bad people down on their luck or donating it to the sorry-fuck owners of the Winnemucca Inn wasn't very appealing. The bigger challenge was that I didn't just get my appetite back for overcooked beef and lamb-sized baked potatoes, I wanted to get laid. Southern Idaho and Utah had attractive women, but their good Mormon values excluded any acquaintance with a connoisseur of the clitoris like myself. They were dry states for me in more ways than one.

I surveyed the opportunities and my choices were young and skanky or old and skankier, each with their respective scars from life wandering the parking lot and rent by the hour rooms. I'd considered just going back to my room and jerking off, but therein lies the problem. Spirit of full disclosure, Larry, and something you don't ever need to mention to a single fucking soul—I have never masturbated. Ever. I'd joke about jerking off often—it's what boys and young men do. But the thought of simulating something myself that was so easy to obtain through

THE LAST LETTER

the natural order of things has always been appalling to me— confirmation of failure to acquire.

By the time there were nights that I had no available options with the ease of a phone call or a stopover, I realized I hadn't ever learned how to do it. I'd assumed the process was simple, so I experimented. After a minute or two of frantic tugging it just seemed pointless and without merit, and definitely didn't feel very good. I had no patience to teach myself and if there is a technique I was too old by then to ask a friend how it's done. If you don't have answers to that question by the time you're around 13, you're never to ask again.

Then it hit me. I'm dying. I'm not going to masturbate. But—big theatrical pause here--I've never been with a prostitute. Like a brick hit me. Like a high-speed chase. A new box to check. Pay a woman for sex. How hard could it be? There were women trawling around, so it should be as easy as picking the naughtiest looking one—like picking a new and untried animal part to eat at a bazaar in Tanzania, which I've done countless times in countless places. Might like it. Might get sick. But, you never know until that first, timid bite. Spoiler alert— most anything anywhere tastes a lot like chicken.

Lucky for me, it was Winnemucca. Prostitution is not only legal, I think it's encouraged, maybe even taught in school. I didn't have to pick. The ladies of the night here are here for business. Before I finished that first JD and Coke, I had three wander up to me asking if I was looking for company. Nope. For fucks sake no. And, the third, I'd only consider after I was completely fucking dead. It seemed like I was up to bat and all the pitches were thrown in the dirt, with plenty of scuff marks on the ball and more than a little pine tar.

Then Tawny—yes, like the fine port I've finished many

an expensive dinner with—showed up. Like the smartass mother-fucker I am, I asked if that was her real name and she responded, "It is tonight." Well, Tawny threw a pitch right down the middle there. Loved the pitch, but wasn't ready to hit it.

I told her I was interested, but I'd never been with a prostitute before and since she did this for a living I was afraid I wouldn't be able to satisfy her. She said, "Oh, you won't satisfy me, Honey, but you WILL please me." Damn, slider that hit the outside corner. She just about had me.

I asked her what I'd get for what I had. She listed off a menu of options and prices like Bob fucking Barker on The Price Is Right. It was Prostitute Plinko. Then, she paused and said, "A fella like you doesn't come around too often. I'm sure I can throw in a few bonus rounds on the house." Shit, the change up. Left me staring. I was in. Hell yes, I was in. She had me. I asked the bartender for their best bottle of wine and two glasses. He came back with a screw top bottle and a twelve-dollar tab. Jesus Christ, it's Winnemucca.

We walked through the half-empty, smoke-filled casino to the elevator and up to the third floor. As we were treading across the sticky, stained hallway carpet to my room, my curiosity caught the best of me. I wanted to learn more about this prostitute thing and was in the process of paying for the education. I started with, "So, how many guys have you been with tonight?". The affable Tawney responded, "Guys? Just you, Honey." Seemed like a stretch. I followed with, "How many hours do you 'work'?" and "What's the best part and worst part of your job?". Seemed like a good opportunity to search the depths of a cave I'd never thought of exploring before.

Tawny quickly grew impatient and went from sultry skank

to simply a young woman with a job and a customer asking too many questions.

"Are you sure you want to do this, mister?" The change in tone and tenor was abrupt and took me off guard.

"Chill, woman named after fortified wine. I'll pay you regardless, and we'll figure it out. I was just interested in what you do for a living."

Immediately, she switched back into the raccoon-eyed mascara seductress I met at the bar, "It's not what I do, but what I'm going to do to YOU. What do you want me to do, Honey?" Seems like possession by multiple personalities is one of the requirements of this particular vocation.

Once we got in my room, the reality hit me. I still had plenty of mojo left and miles to cover so I'd certainly get laid again before I die. Cancer sucks, but the thought of giving some good-minded, free-thinking attractive woman cooties from a whore in Winnemucca created a sense of guilt I couldn't get past.

As she was slowly rubbing her palms against her breasts and ass, occasionally stopping front side for a quick between the legs massage and making a lot of "ooh" and "ahh" sounds— all while completely clothed and, not for her being a hooker, somewhat hot—the brick hit me again. I was with a "sexpert". I had never learned to masturbate. I had cash and she had knowledge. Knowledge I needed more than herpes or syphilis.

I made my own proposition: I'd pay her what she'd make from a blowjob and hard fuck if she taught me how to masturbate and, as for my bonus rounds she could show me how she masturbated. I did mention it would help if she was undressed. Gnarly as she may have been—she had front teeth that could open a tin can of tomato soup, and oddly pistol-grip-shaped ears--she did have a fucking killer body.

Larry, what happened next was one of the most honest and thoughtful interactions I've ever had with a woman. She dropped both the working girl pseudo-sultriness and the skank pretense. She was tender and unassuming. Patient. Kind. She was an able teacher and I was a curious, willing student. I learned to masturbate--very well, mind you. And, nearing the end of an hour, I did so again during her exhibition of techniques of female self-pleasure that I couldn't have imagined before last night. It was money well spent, and well earned.

We sat for a moment in the room staring at each other with the calm smile of satisfaction that is usually reserved for cats that eat canaries. She asked if I was staying in town and I told her I was just passing through. "Too bad.", she said, pointing at my package, "I'd be willing to give you a freebie just to see how all that works in real life." I did give it a thought. I shook my head and said, "Tempting as it is, Darlin', and as good as I assure you it would be, I doubt you could afford it." I'm not sure any man has been able to muster a genuine laugh from a pussy-for-hire, but I'm sure that's as close as a genuine laugh can be between a prostitute and a John. The student had become the master. Or, in this case, the master baiter.

I tried my newfound skill this morning. Still a few adjustments to make, but I figure if I die with my dick in my hand at least they'll say, "He was doing what he loved.", not realizing I had just learned to do it and, while not loving it, making a pretty good go of it.

That phrase, "He died doing what he loved" is such bullshit, by the way. I've summited five of the seven summits with some of the grittiest bastards you'd ever meet. I've spent the night bivvying while hypothermic on rock walls on multi-pitch climbs. I've skied backcountry bowls dodging avalanches twice. I've lost some very good friends doing it all. Strong people in heart, soul, and mind that had no fucking business dying. At the funerals, people would always say, "He was doing what he loved." Fuck that. Nobody loves dying. They definitely didn't love dying when they did it. I'm dying now, and I fucking hate it. My grandpa died of a heart attack while he was on the toilet. You think he loved that? No. People don't die doing what they love or they wouldn't be dead. They live and just happen to be unlucky enough to die at any particular and random time. Time to sign off and get this to the post office while I'm still pissed off thinking about it. I have a long drive this afternoon to wherever I end up, and I'll get plenty of miles in thinking of how cancer is going to fuck me out of all this.

Give Debbie and the kids my regards. And, always close your eyes—quality masturbation is 90% mental and 10% technique. Take it from Tawny, the girl named after dessert wine.

*Stroke On,
Tracy*

The abrupt change in tone of Tracy's voice at the end of the tape startled me. He was angry, and it came without warning. I had wondered if and when the reality of certain death would become clear to him, as he did tend to be emotionally obtuse at times. His anger seemed to reflect one of the seven stages of loss, the first and most important stage. Yet, my time was up and I needed to transition to my own life. My real life. It was time to head back to the house and tuck the kids in before bed. A strange transition from the half-hour diatribe on the details of prostitution and masturbation in the desert of Nevada, but a transition I have been learning to make with efficiency and expediency when the kitchen alarm finally sounds.

On a cold and snowy Sunday the kids were inside watching TV and Debbie seemed quite settled in her sewing room. Winter days like this are lazy days. The clock ticks slower as the snow drifts outside. I had an opportunity for extra time in the shop and I took it. I set my timer for two hours and decided to go deep, as they say, and work through as many letters and tapes as I could.

Based on the postmarks and letters, Tracy oscillated north and south through the Sierras like a seismograph. His letters tended to focus on the natural beauty of the area, reminiscences of past adventures and the people and lessons he learned from them, and several rolls of film. The tone and content of each letter seemed to oscillate, as well. I could see it from the points on the map and the points made in each subsequent letter that there was the pressure of the two geologic plates of life and death pushing against each other until, at some point, there would be a major earthquake. A reset.

The outburst at the end of the Winnemucca tape was the first foreshadowing. A subtle sign of things to come. While I could sense it, I could not accurately predict when it would happen and what the damage would be.

After around eight or ten envelopes there was another cardboard parcel with a tape in it. The postmark was Willow Creek, California. The challenge with tapes is the length. Some have been very short—five minutes or so—and others

THE LAST LETTER

have been meandering tomes that often take the full thirty minutes that a miniature Memorex tape can hold. I usually listen all the way through, then go through another couple of times to transcribe. I have been successful transcribing within an hour regardless of the length of the soliloquy, but only because it is a learned behavior due to my self-imposed sixty-minute constraint. The Willow Creek tape was a long story, and well worth recounting.

Dear Larry,

Today started like many of the days of the past few weeks. I was camped off a forest service road that followed the Cal Salmon River in the middle of the Trinity Alps. I'd rafted both the Cal Salmon and Klamath Rivers years ago and I was happy to return. It's a remote area just outside the four-house town of Somes Bar. It's the very best of the Golden Bear state.

I packed up and continued west. I had a challenge. The last gas station was two hours east and I was certain the next one was two hours west. Not an issue unless your gas tank runs around three hours in the mountains and you're sitting on Empty.

I'd been here before and knew Humboldt County's claim to fame isn't the wild and scenic rivers and the lush, verdant mountainsides of harvestable pines. Humboldt County is the largest pot-producing county in these United States. There aren't many people in these woods and the ones that are here grow weed on a large scale, and guard their plots with heavy munitions. I was warned of such on one of my rafting trips on the Cal Salmon.

You don't venture too far off a paved road, and definitely don't want to stumble upon a plot or you're bound to get shot and chopped up for fertilizer. I'm fucking serious. Like American Werewolf in London—"Stay on road. Stay out of the moors." Except these "moors" are heavily guarded forests thick with pine and high-grade pot.

People don't live here because they want to host family reunions in the scenic wilds of the Trinity's. They live here because they don't want to be found. They're off-the-gridders that want to be left way the fuck alone.

Well, I was about out of gas and figurin' I was fucked since it was a Wednesday and there probably wouldn't be any rafters or campers rolling down Salmon River Road anytime soon. I wouldn't have much more luck if I made it to highway 96. I made it fifteen minutes with my gas needle on "E". I saw a shack down a steep lane off 96 and thought I'd try my luck. Sure, there's a nest of Unabombers in that shack, but if they have a few gallons of unleaded I was willing to pay a premium for it and be on my way.

I pulled up and got off the bike. Not a fucking soul in sight, but about six big ass dogs on fucking Cujo chains surrounded the property. These fuckers weren't rescued from the pound, they eat what people rescue from the pound. I shouted out to see if anyone was there. Like knowing there are mean bears in the woods, your best bet is always to make as much noise as you can so you don't startle them, and so they think you're too fucking stupid to want to attack. Loud, noisy people aren't a threat, there a nuisance.

There were old trucks and a couple of World War II-era jeeps around the property and a shack that looked like a shithole with old timbers for walls and a sheet metal roof. There was a large shed, and where there's a shed there has to be petroleum. I wandered around the edges of the barking dogs like I was slowly maneuvering through a mine field like Kwai Chang Caine walking the rice paper carpet in Kung Fu and made it to the shed.

Just as I got to the door, I heard, "Hold it right fucking there." Had a feeling it wasn't a representative from the Burnt Mattress, California Chamber of Commerce, so I froze and slowly raised my hands. Always raise your hands. I turned around and about twelve feet away was a grizzly-looking fucker with an old leather hat, a raggedy flannel shirt under bib overalls, and a thick gray beard.

He was kind of a cross between Miner 49'er from Scooby Do and Rusty from ZZ Top. And, of course, he had a fucking shotgun pointed at me. Honestly, why does everyone west of the Missouri River have to have a fucking shotgun and the liberty to point it at well-intended people like me? I'm so fucking tired of shotguns and their propensity to be beaded in on my cancer-ridden abdomen!

Anyway, I slowly took my helmet off and told him I was about out of gas and just needed a few gallons and was willing to pay anything for it. Then the interrogation started in earnest. "Where the fuck are you from?", "What are you fucking doing out here?", "How could you run out of gas?", "You work for the government?", "Anybody know you're here?". It took about ten questions that he didn't bother for me to answer before he asked why I was snooping around his barn and pissing his dogs off.

I told him I was looking for the owner of the property, hoped it was him, and would just need some gas if he could spare it and be on my way.

"That your bike over there?" When a backwoods fuck has a gun pointed at you, you can't be a smartass, although the temptation was killing me. Of course it was my bike, Captain

Dumbfuck. I opted for the more congenial, "It sure is. The bike and everything in it. And, it's got no gas and that's the only business I have here."

He walked up to me, un-cocked his twelve-gauge, and put out his hand, "Name's Randy. I can get some gas for you, but you'll need to be on your way. I don't do visitors, especially the uninvited kind."

Randy pulled open the sliding barn door and told me I could come inside. There were large sheets of plastic around the walls and across the rafters. It was a drying barn and there were stalks of premium Northern California ganja hanging from wire lines like an upside-down forest. Randy, it turns out, was a farmer and a businessman.

I laughed and said, "Jesus Christ, Randy, this all yours? This is fucking awesome!" Even a paranoid hemp grower is proud of his wares so that seemed to disarm him. It's amazing how many jams I've gotten out of with a laugh and a 'fucking awesome'. I could tell he wanted to show me around, but I realized real quick that the only thing worse than stumbling across a pot processing barn was being in a pot processing barn if Johnny Q. Law showed up. I just wanted my gas and to get the fuck out of there. I kept looking around the barn looking for a can of gas, while he was starting the grand tour.

He asked if it was too early to have a drink, and I told him I had a lot of driving to do and had a flask with some good Jack Daniels in it for when the hankering hit me. Also told him my stomach's not in great shape for early morning drinking.

He said, "Jack Daniels is trash whiskey. Let me fill your flask with some good stuff." Well, that's an offer I could accept. He walked me around the back of the shed and there was a wood pile with a lean-to extended from the barn and, to my *surprise, a fully operational still with shelves full of old glass gallon jugs with clear liquid. Turns out Randy was a pot farmer and moonshiner and at that point, I figured I'd risk a run-in with the law to learn more. He grabbed a couple of old glasses off the shelf and poured us each a half a glass. "Try this.", Randy said as he handed the glass to me.*

"Is this gas for my bike, or for me to drink? Looks like some pretty mean shit."

Randy laughed and said I could use it for both, but he double-charcoal filters it so it's smooth as a super model's ass. Doesn't give you a hangover. Hell, now I had no choice. I took a sip and it was pretty damn good, but it burned all the way down to my fucking toes.

We took our moonshine back into the shed and he pulled out a bench and sat down. Amazing what a little moonshine will do to open up a good conversation with a rusty-assed redneck. Randy told me he used to work for the forest service and settled into his place about twenty years ago. He learned how to grow pot and keep it out of sight from the law with a few well-guarded plots in the thick canopy of the forest. "Can't even see my plots from the choppers!", he proudly boasted. We kept sipping and he kept talking.

He told me he had a "crew of injuns" from the nearby Hoopla reservation that guarded his plots with grenades and machine guns.

"They're meaner than a bag of snakes, and work for a little cash and a lot of whiskey. And, best of all, they have a genuine spite for lawmen."

Seemed reasonable enough.

"I got a bunch of injun women that come in to pack and

process every couple a weeks. If you stick around another week or so, stop on by, it's a hell of a sight to see."

I thought if I'd asked about his distribution model or client base—the ad agency man in me was curious—the conversation would end with me floating face down in the Klamath River to meet the waves of the Pacific. The old phrase, "It doesn't hurt to ask.", is rarely the case, and certainly wasn't applicable here. I was damn sure I'd be hurt if I asked.

We finally got around to me. He asked, again, where I was from. In situations like this, the last fucking thing you want to tell people is "Chicago". I stayed with "Oh, I'm a Midwest boy. A flatlander, damn us all!" He liked that. I had a why the fuck not moment and told him about my cancer and my goal to get to the coast. "Too many people.", he said, asking pensively, "Why would you want to die around all them damn people." There was no "Sorry to hear that.", or, "That's too bad." I think he figured he had his life and I had mine and we both had better sense than to question the motives of the other.

We went for a refill on the moonshine and I told him I'd probably had enough because my stomach is a little tender and I still had to make it through the mountains. He asked what I was taking for my stomach and I listed most of the contents of my mobile medicine cabinet. "That's all shit, friend. Well, except the Vicodin. That's good stuff. What you need is some high-grade Randy hybrid. My own brand. Cross between Purple Kush and Blue Dream. Took me years to get it just right."

Hell, I wasn't with Randy, I was with Karl Spangler from fucking Caddyshack!

He pulled open an old metal cabinet and gave me an enormous fucking bag of the shit, proudly exclaiming, "Best weed in the entire state!". I said, "Well, Randy, I appreciate it and all, but I don't have a lot of cash and honestly I'm not much of a smoker. Hell, I don't even know how to roll a joint."

Randy responded, "I don't want your damn money. Hell, do I look like I need money?"

Spoiler alert, Larry, he did look like he needed the money, but why stop a generous man on a mission of charity?

"Here, I'll give you a one-hitter and show you the ropes." He handed me a small pipe loaded with premium weed. Within two minutes of that one smoother than it should have been hit, my stomach was tingling and my mind was at ease. While I'm not thrilled with having a pound of contraband in my back trunk, it was an offer I couldn't refuse.

I told Randy I felt bad not being able to give him something in return. Didn't take him long—and four hits of his own weed—for him to circle back to the Vicodin. "You ever snort that stuff?", he asked. "Nope. Doctor never put that on the prescription pad.", I said. He told me Vicodin is the poor man's cocaine. Well, I could definitely get behind a good line of coca-cola, so I let him go on.

We went out to my bike, grabbed my family-sized bottle of Vicodin and I gave him a few dozen. We went back and he crushed one up. He had a fucking mortar and pestle. Who the fuck has a mortar and pestle? A pine forest drug lord, of course. He crushed one up and drew up a few lines on the glass top of an old desk. He rolled up a c-note and told me to be careful—only start with a half a line.

Jesus. Between the moonshine, the spleef, and the Vicodin-as-cocaine line, I felt like I was at the Disneyland of drugs and each ride just kept getting more fun. I started with It's a Small

World moved to Pirates of the Caribbean, then screamed down Magic Mountain. God, it felt good. No, it felt great.

He told me if shit gets too real, I could cook the Vicodin on a spoon—just like heroin—and put a few drops in a glass of moonshine. "You don't even taste it.", he said. I told him I wasn't into heroin or needles, but I appreciated the good advice. "One last thing, friend.", he said, getting serious as a heart attack, "Don't do more than a couple drops out of that spoon or it will kill you." Not quite sure how scientific his discovery was, but he wasn't dead so I guess he found the "just enough without being too much" dose.

After my two hours with Randy, I finally got my two gallons of gas and a flask full of double charcoal filtered moonshine. I shook his hand and told him it was a damn fine morning for me. "They all are." Randy said and laughed, closing with, "Every day is a good day up here, even the bad ones." Just before waving me off, he said, "Good luck with your dyin' thing."

I made it to Willow Creek to fill up and ate more than I had in weeks at a local Dairy Queen. I'm going to get this to the post office and head across 299 to the coast.

Larry, there are more good people out there than people think. Randy's good people. Odd as fuck, as many can be, but good people. I got lucky today and am anxious to get to the coast.

Give Debbie and the kids a big hug for me. And, if they want to vacation in northern California, take them to the real Disneyland instead.

A Friend With Weed Is A Friend Indeed,
Tracy

CHAPTER 11

GOD, WOMEN, AND THE HEALING POWER OF WATER

The next envelope was another tape and I was thankful to have the extra hour to go through it. I only had time to listen through once. I had just lit a second cigarette with the tape playing, and I realized a minute into it that this was the reset I had been wondering about. I took the cigarette out of my mouth, leaned back in my chair, closed my eyes, and just listened as the smoke quietly rose from my carburetor turned ashtray.

Larry,

I'm sitting by a driftwood fire on the California coast halfway between an incoming high tide and a tree line laden with redwoods and firs. It is remote. Not another soul for miles. Just the warmth of a late-day sun, large rocks littering the inlet, and the sound of the tide crashing in like thunder and slowly rolling back against the rocks on the beach like a broom loudly sweeping time itself. The yin and yang of the crashing waves and their eerie, rolling retreat are mesmerizing. The waves are timeless, flowing before life existed, and long after life will end. The vastness of the ocean is on full display here. The only horizon is a subtle shift of blue shades from water to sky. I am small here. Inconsequential. And, I love it.

The view is even better than the hypnotic cadence of the waves. Powerful better. I can close my eyes and see it just as vividly as when they're open. The changing hues of blue as the sun draws to the watery horizon versus the dark, grey shadows of the cliffs and large rocks that are randomly littered across the inlet can't be painted in a picture, or captured in a camera—I'm not even going to try to take pictures. I can't describe it well enough. You're so much better at that than I am. I wish I could do better. I wish you could see this and explain it in a manner it best deserves. Behind me are cliffs dotted with giant redwoods, fir, and spruce mixed among huge ferns and wild grasses sprouting from the spongy soil.

I've surfed and spear-fished in the ocean many times.

THE LAST LETTER

Spearing is my favorite thing to do. It's like hunting in the Midwest, but without dogs or spraying deer piss all over you and sitting in a stand. It's more intimate. You're one with the sea. Patient. When you slowly dive down for a shot, all you can feel is your heartbeat and the teaming sea life around you. You're in their rhythm, their world. Then, the rush of the fight to reel your line to take them from their world to yours. It's Zen as fuck.

Today there was no spear. No five mil wet suit. Just me diving into eight-foot waves before they crashed so I could feel the rush of the foam and water across my back. For a few minutes, I thought of letting the sea take me out, which seemed like a perfect ending. Like I would turn into Aquaman and return to the sea with new life, new powers, and no cancer. The escape was tempting, but the reality was that I'd end up washing up on shore bloated and shitty looking with maggots tearing through my carcass. No fucking thanks. I spent an hour in the frigid waters completely free, then walked back to shore to build this fire and appreciate a view that few are lucky enough to ever see.

Incredible. Just fucking incredible. I have always viewed every day as a gift, even more so now. I've never subscribed to the "Is the glass half empty, or half full?" bullshit. I've just been glad to have the glass. Even waking up vomiting until I nearly pass out, waking up for another day is a gift. Randy was right, Larry, "Every day is a good day. Even the bad ones.", and this day just happens to be better than most.

God made this place, Larry, and I don't say that lightly. My relationship with the Almighty has been rocky most of my life and it's time to clear a few things up with him. I want to share it with you, too, because I've always respected your devotion to your God and your Savior, even though I've never fully subscribed myself. He may need to be my only witness, but having you along shouldn't hurt. Bet he won't mind.

My first recollection of organized religion was in Phoenix. I was placed in St. Agnes daycare and pre-school when I was four. I was different. While the other kids were eating paste-- tastes better than it should, by the way--and putting glitter and glue on pictures of Jesus, I was learning to read and write. I couldn't get enough. But—like most of my life—I had a hard time sitting still and keeping quiet in class. While most of the other sisters were tolerant, Sister Fan was not.

Sister Fan—Pam Fan, if you can fucking believe someone would name their kid that--would tell me that God wants us to be obedient, and talking to others in class isn't part of God's plan. Based on class pictures that are etched in my memory, Sister Fan was in her early 30's and likely went to the convent because only God could appreciate her homeliness. The good Lord might have loved her, but no way a man would. Her preferred method of conveying God's will for obedience was a ruler across your knuckles when you'd talk in class. I swear I still have the numbers two through six tattooed under the skin of my knuckles.

One early summer day when I was five I came home and my mom asked me why my knuckles were marked and bloody. I told her. She immediately pulled me out of St. Agnes pre-school in July and I started second grade in August when I was five. They didn't test back then, but the principal of Papago Elementary said I'd long passed the requirements of those first couple grades. I always hated being the youngest, smallest kid in school, and I've never forgiven God and his minion, Sister Fan, for making that happen.

THE LAST LETTER

I went to the Christian Church in town with Grandma Bea a couple times a month when I was in high school, but it was mainly because I knew she liked it when I joined her. By then, I'd already done enough sinning on a regular basis that no Sunday hymnals were going to be able to wash that sin away.

In college, I tried the Catholic church again. It seemed like they had the best approach--sinning during the week with an hour of good repentance listening to Father Steve on Sunday to clear the ledger for Monday. Plus, there were a ton of hot chicks that attended the Catholic church and nothing draws women like the prospect of a man making the effort to be holy and righteous while knowing they'd fail every time. The potential for changing a man, especially a sinful man, is an unearthly draw for any woman.

I'd formed a pretty good relationship with God Thy Father, Creator of Heaven and Earth. I accepted I was a heathen, and knew he agreed, but I was putting forth the effort in trying to be a better person and I figured He appreciated that. I made it a point to hit mass in Chicago those first few years even when a tough Sunday hangover made my sacrifice in attending more than the other, better people in the pews.

This was all shits and grins until Grandma Bea got sick. I struggled. How could a just and merciful God bring such pain and punishment to the most decent person I'd ever met? My guardian angel. There are always one or two people in your life that enter into it and change the course of your destiny for the better. That either rescue you or provide the opportunity for you to rescue yourself. Grandma Bea was my guardian angel, and she went through hell at the end.

As she went through her treatments, each worse than the next, I read the Bible cover to cover—twice. If it was the word of God, and God was all-merciful and all-knowing and loving, there had to be something in there about how to save a perfect soul. I always got stuck on the Book of Job. It reminded me of my Grandma. God wasn't merciful and loving at all, not to those that earned it, anyway. There were no answers in the Bible—not a single damn one--and I've since viewed it as a collection of short stories transcribed over hundreds of years from fables, and translated by corrupt men with motives of their own.

At her funeral, the thought of memorializing her in a house built to honor a clearly unjust God was more than I could take. I walked straight out, got in my car, and drove home. I stopped off interstate 80 around What Cheer and vomited. The rest of the drive I talked to God. Literally, in my car, had a one- way conversation—he didn't talk back. I told him I was done with him. That I would hold no grudge, but that he could have his and I'd have mine. He would no longer be a part of my life, and he wouldn't have to worry about me from then on. I was no longer one of his children. I didn't forsake him for others. I didn't turn to Buddhism, Hinduism, Islam, or Shinto, although there are components of them all that I do subscribe to.

Her funeral was the last time I have ever set foot in a house of worship. I've been to plenty of weddings since, but have never gone to the ceremony if it was in a church. That being said, I've never ever missed a good reception.

My parents didn't sway me either way. My dad has tried to believe, but he is too much of a doubter. His thought has always been that when you die that's just the end and there's nothing after, so there is no need for an afterlife-offering deity. We have argued about it often--when I was more Godly, and since. In my mind, we all come back in some way. And, the things we do here on earth follow us from one life to the next. My mom has rarely attended church, choosing instead to soothe her soul in other ways—some with success, many without. Katie and Tom are good Christian folk, but they know my position and have always seemed to respect it.

Whether I'd climb mountains or a rock face, God was never a part of it. Most climbers aren't Christians or really religious at all. They don't want to put their fate in a deity. Your fate when you climb is a combination of an eleven-millimeter diameter poly rope and a locked carabiner, your climbing partners, a good ice ax, and a complete focus on the face of the rock. A little luck helps, and God would just get in the way. Even when I'd get to the top and—the hardest part—successfully back down, God wasn't with me. I've had more faith in my climbing party than I've ever had in God. If I didn't have that complete faith at the start of a climb, I wouldn't climb. And, when I would get back to the bottom without injury, I'd always thank the team, not God. We'd share a special moment, but not with Him.

I always thought that God never created the beauty of the rock or the incredible vistas that are your reward for the effort. It was geology, carved over millions of years with millions more to go. Our agreement that day in the car seemed to work very well until today.

Here I am. Staring at a picture that goes beyond geology. Beyond ice ages and volcanoes that carve and build beautiful landscapes. There is too much life here at this moment than I've ever seen on any rock face or the summit of any peak. I feel a part of it. A small, insignificant part.

No, God is life. And, life is love. And love is peace. I'm doing a shitty job of explaining it, but I do feel the presence of God—around me and within me. An abundance of life. I feel it in my heart, and it feels rich and bountiful. There is a God, and God is good. I shouldn't have blamed God for taking good people from me.

I should have been thankful he put those guardian angels in my life at just the right time to help me course-correct and savor the love and acceptance they provided to me—love and acceptance that I am now convinced He provided to them so they could share it freely with others and without condition. While I am still a skeptic of organized religion, there is no doubt for me that there is a God and that He or She or It is here with me, and I with Him."

There was a long pause in the tape—probably two to three minutes—where it just played. I could hear the faint sounds of the ocean breaking, birds, and an occasional wisp of mild breeze. I closed my eyes to picture what Tracy was seeing, and ponder what he was feeling while the tape was aimlessly running. I was comforted to know he had finally made peace with his maker after a several-year absence and did so with no minister and no pews--only the pulpit of creation and the beautiful, bountiful circle of life. Then, the dialogue continued:

"I might as well address the other elephant in the room, Larry. My relationships. Or, more accurately, the lack of a lasting relationship like yours and others I witnessed over the years that weren't nearly as successful as you and Debbie. Trust me, as you get through your twenties with no ring on your finger, the subject comes up frequently—particularly with family.

I have loved many women but loved only a few that I felt I could spend the rest of my life with, which is the typical measuring stick for marital consideration. I have broken many hearts and genuinely have felt bad when I've done so, and have had my heart broken three times. A broken heart never fully heals, but it does heal enough to fall in love again. Must be a heart thing. I never resisted the opportunity to fall in love, even knowing the consequences if it didn't work out. The juice has always been worth the squeeze.

I have had relationships—from a few hours to several months—with countless women. Enough experience that I could usually measure up the length of stay in any given relationship within the first ten or fifteen minutes. Sleeping with someone was never a moral compass issue for me, but more of an opportunity for an adventure. If a woman's personality interested me, the more adventure there'd be and the longer it'd last. A killer body helped, even if the woman was an emotional science project that you knew was likely to explode—like introducing nitro to glycerin.

The closest thing I had been given to relationship advice to that point was from my dad. My dad speaks in metaphors and they don't usually make sense, like a Jim Morrison lyric—the beat sure sounds good, but the words can't catch up. Ron told me that there are women that are like roller coasters and others that are like the Amtrak through Kansas. They both ride on tracks but one will make you laugh, scream and cry and the other may bore the hell out of you, but the ride will last a whole lot longer. I only wanted to spend time with the women that did the inverted 360's and a 200-foot drop and rarely had the patience for the Amtrak through Kansas.

I was in love with Rhonda Myers in high school. Hard love, as first loves usually are. It was a good thing that we broke up—or that she broke up with me—because I could have never committed. Not in college. Too many adventures. Plus, Rhonda was determined to live the rest of her life in Pleasantville and she and I both knew that I had no plans to return. We learned love together so it was easier to attach to the commonality of love without needing the foresight of the future.

My second love was Kristen Johnson. That was real love, not just the convenience of high school. Love in college was different because there were so many of the opposite sex to choose from that when you did choose one, it seemed more special. She was more special. She was the first and last soul connection I've ever had. I could have married Kristen, but she either wasn't ready or thought I wasn't ready. She was right either way.

My final true love was Leslie Howard. While I wouldn't call her a soul mate in the proper sense, I've never been so compatible with a woman or—honestly—another human being. She was like me, with perfectly shaped breasts and an incredible ass. I loved her as a human being, a friend, a bedmate, and fellow provocateur. But, I never felt the tingle. The tingle is the key for me.

The tingle comes from your soul—from some place you don't even know about that whispers all the right things into your brain to allow the connection and release all the right hormones. The tingle is the chemistry. Leslie and I had all the makings of a perfectly married couple, except the damn tingle. I was ripped off on that. She would have been perfect if I'd only had the tingle I had with every touch of Kristen's hand and gentle stroke through her blond hair. A light kiss on the tip of her nose created more tingle than a ten-hour sex marathon with Leslie. Yes, Larry, ten hours. Absolutely no exaggeration there.

I'd seen enough people married by then, many unsuccessfully, that I changed my view of love and marriage. I'd always thought you should marry someone you felt you could spend the rest of your life with, not just the rest of the night. I'd seen

THE LAST LETTER

too many people that believed that fallacy only to end up with half their assets and a full set of baggage sometime later after a divorce. If you were meant to spend the rest of your life with a great companion, you could get a dog, if only they lived longer.

I thought it was a fear of commitment, but I never felt any fear at the thought of committing to someone I loved and while I strayed a bit with the three women I've loved deeply, my love for them never strayed one bit—don't get caught up in the contradiction, just go with me on this. It could have been childhood trauma, I thought. While I took a few scrapes and scratches out of all that I've never felt a permanent wound that would make me a serial philanderer.

It was coming up in conversation often enough and I didn't have any sort of answer, so I went to a therapist to see what the issue might be. One caveat with a therapist—figure it out within 3 sessions, or we're done. Therapists are like chiropractors in that regard, and I had no appetite for months of therapy digging up dragons I'd slain long ago.

Within two sessions the good Dr. John McBride was able to focus on two things, and I will share them both with you. First, it was all shits and grins with women—conquests, love, maybe love, fun, a little heartbreak—until my Grandma Bea died. Her death awakened me to both the seriousness and shortness of life, as well as the fragility. The loss I felt when she died was so strong and so permanent that I developed an intense fear of fucking losing someone I loved again. Best way to avoid the loss was to refuse the gain. That one's definitely on me.

Fear will fight the battle against love and win more often than it loses. All love offers is truth. Fear has many more tools of deceit and denial at its disposal, and I tended to use them all. Like so many of my life's lessons, I learned that one too well and too late. I regret it.

Second, and probably more importantly, Dr. John said I had an unreasonable definition of true love. It was unreasonable because in my mind it was—and still is—non-negotiable. My definition is the standard on which any loving relationship I have approached is ultimately measured against, and probably why each of them has all ultimately ended.

There's a big difference in my mind between love and being in love. You can love someone deeply enough to spend the rest of your life together. But being in love means that you want to spend every fucking minute of the rest of your life with them. Loving them more than yourself. Being in love is being willing to take a bullet for her not because you want to die, but because you can't bear the thought of living without her.

Being in love is being the same soul in two different bodies that just happen, usually by chance, to wander into each other only to be separated by space or time, but never separated in spirit--not in this world or the next.

The good doctor McBride told me that my version of 'in love' was common early in relationships and that after the hormones die down, as they eventually will, you need more threads in the fabric. Essentially saying it wasn't sustainable. Dr. John was wrong. I've met women I could enjoy the rest of my life with. I've met women that are such good people I'd take a bullet for them. But, Larry, I've never met a woman that I was in love with to the point where every time I saw her—whether we were apart for a few minutes or a few days, wouldn't matter--I'd either feel like the first time our eyes met or like we were taking our last, best breath together.

I realize it's too late to try now. I don't fear losing someone

THE LAST LETTER

now that my life is almost lost. I do fear the lost opportunity for true love. For being in love. I would like to feel the tingle one last time, but that's just not how this dying thing works. I definitely got gypped on that.

Thanks for letting me get that off my chest, Larry. It was like a couple of albatrosses circling me the past several weeks constantly trying to shit on me. I needed someone besides me to know I've reconciled with both God and women. I found God again, and accept that I won't have the chance to find love. I was able to reconcile with both because I was immersed in the beauty and grandeur of God on a perfect afternoon on the California Coast.

Time to go back in the water before it gets too dark so I can heal my soul with a few big waves. Cancer can stop my heart, but it can't kill my soul. I'm heading to Palo Alto from here for some unfinished business, then to scale a few big faces one last time while I still can in Yosemite.

Give my regards to Debbie. You two have looked in love every time I've seen you and that's damn rare. You'd take that bullet for each other, without hesitation. I imagine you know that.

Until Zen,
Tracy

This tape was the only one that I came back to the shop to listen to for the next few sessions, and I'm not sure why I paused my progress to contemplate my own relationship with God and my Savior, as well as my relationship with Debbie. I was raised Presbyterian, the common man's Protestantism. I have never had the wonder or wherewithal to question my maker, it is simply something Presbyterians do not do. My faith has provided me with comfort and counsel that I have also been able to impress upon my own children, just as it was impressed upon me by my parents and their parents before them.

In a similar vein, my relationship with my wife is a covenant with God that I willingly and gladly stepped into, thanking Him for bringing us together. We have been fortunate to share both the same deep and committed love to our Lord as we have in each other. The two are one in the same. God created love between a man and a woman who share their love for God and with Him.

In essence, I feel very similarly to Tracy regarding his current interpretation of God and—to some extent—love, and have always felt fortunate to have been introduced to both very early in my life. I do not understand how an atheistic misogynist and a life-long Christian with a single committed love could arrive at a similar place in such very different ways. In that lies evidence of the mystery of God and the mystery of love, and neither are mine to question.

CHAPTER 12
THE PITCH AND THE PARTY IN PALO ALTO

A week had passed and it was time to move on for both Tracy, and for me. His journals—whether written or verbal—were starting to follow a familiar pattern. There would be several letters detailing random and often humorous tales of each day, followed by a day or two pause, then a deeper disclosure into transformations that are better left acknowledged or understood prior to passing. There would be another few day pause, then the details of a grand adventure. Then more concurrent daily accounts from his time on the road: The people he would meet, the things he would see, and the occasional inclusion of pictures to better frame the experiences.

He provided great detail on the progression of his symptoms and how he was managing them or failing to do so. While his health had not yet failed, it was obvious it was in decline, and that decline was accelerating. Describing such decline and accepting it are two different things, however, so he would provide the detail with no acknowledgment of the cause—always the symptoms, never the disease. There was no sense of possession. It was never "my" cancer or "my" symptoms, but second-person accounts like how most people would describe a neighbor or a tree. He hadn't yet taken ownership of the monster inside him. Frankly, I am not sure it is something I would want to accept in that situation either. Describing a malady instead of owning it makes it less real, and his reality was one few would choose to face.

The last tape he made was from a Holiday Inn in Palo Alto, California, and was a menagerie worth sharing verbatim. His pace was tired but quick, almost rushed. He clearly had his next destination in mind while he recorded his last.

Larry,

THE LAST LETTER

I'm dictating from the luxury of a Holiday Inn Holidome off Highway 82 in Palo Alto. I'd considered staying in downtown San Fran at one of my favorite hotels, the Fairmont in Ghirardelli Square, for a well-earned night of luxury accommodation after several days wandering the wilds of the northern California coast. But, I looked damn road-weary and it was time for a laundry break and neither would be acceptable at the Fairmont. Holiday Inns are the simple man's hotel—clean, washers and dryers available, and no questions as long as your credit card clears.

I loaded the washer with my clothes, took stock of my gear, and looked in the mirror. I needed to clean up and was in definite need of a night in civilization. My whole purpose in coming to Palo Alto was to have a last few hours of rugby on one of my favorite pitches on the planet, Steuber Stadium, on the campus of Stanford University. It's a simple pitch with small, dingy stands where people can watch some of the best rugby played in the United States.

I've played there three times. A full-side match with the Chicago Lions; a Sevens tournament on a Midwest Select team a year later; and, a 15's tournament playing for Chicago last year. The first day of that last tournament I was a full-on assassin playing the best rugby of my life as if I could will opponents into submission. I saw the game in slow motion and my stamina and penchant for destruction were at their peak. I had reached "the zone", and it was incredible.

Before every rugby game begins, both team captains meet at mid-field with the referee to discuss ball possessions, rule interpretation (referees have license to police at their preference), and injury substitutions. The substitution agreement is key.

You can agree to no substitutions, or up to two substitutions for injury per game.

If you believe it will be a particularly rough game, you want full substitution rights. If you think your team will be more physical but may have less stamina, you go for no subs—you don't want your opponent to be able to bring in fresh legs late in a game. It's a chess match and a little like betting on horses in a race, except there are fifteen horses per side.

After the mid-field meeting before the start of our last game on the first day, I was the captain. I felt we had a hell of an edge over a team from Boston and elected for no substitutions. I came back to the boys in the huddle and told them, reminding them that if they could stand up, they could play. Playing with a cripple on the field is better than playing a man or two short—the gaps in play get much bigger.

Late in that last game of the first day, I broke two ribs. I actually heard them break more than I felt them, and based on the crowd response, they heard it, too. It's very distinct. About five minutes later, I definitely felt the pain, and felt it intensely. There were no subs, so there was no way I was leaving the game. I could run and kick, but the hits were punishing. I finished the game, but for the first time in years had a noticeable vulnerability.

My roster of bumps, bruises, and breaks over eleven years of rugby is long—a twice-broken nose, a broken ankle, three broken fingers with a ripped tendon that will never heal, a separated shoulder, a minor ligament tear, a couple dozen randomly placed stitches, and two concussions.

The ankle and shoulder both kept me out a few games—I sawed my ankle cast off after three impatient weeks, which was a mistake—it still affects me at inconvenient times. I never had an issue playing with pain as long as I could compensate with performance and, occasionally, a few pain pills. The ribs were different. Heading into Sunday's games I felt like there was a target on my chest and for the first time, I tried to guard my injury from hard contact.

One of our coaches, Lanny Watkins--a nearly toothless, short Welshman with thin red hair--pulled me aside during the five-minute halftime of that first game on Sunday and asked if I wanted to finish the tournament on the women's pitch. "All due respect, Lanny, fuck you.", I told him, "They know my ribs are busted and they're fucking crushing me." Then, Lanny gave me the best advice regarding pain and fear I'd ever heard and still live by to this day.

"Lad, fear has no place on the pitch. Fear leads to hesitation, and hesitation leads to injury—both for you and for the other lads on the team. If you can't attack, don't walk back onto that pitch. The best remedy for pain is to provide it to others."

I finished the game. Every loose ruck, maul, and tackle felt like knife blades going through my chest. Each time it just pissed me off more and made me hit harder and run faster. I ended up with a mild lung puncture—there's an oxymoron for you--and coughed a little blood for several days after, but learned an invaluable lesson. I turned fear into anger and anger into performance. I passed the test. I knew I couldn't play the rest of the tournament as soon as the game ended.

After the game, Lanny had two of the guys that weren't on the roster for the rest of the day take me to the hospital with strict instructions to return to the hotel after and not go to any bars. Lanny was wise to me and knew that's exactly where I'd go. After X-rays and the verdict, I asked the ER doc, young guy named Tom Hart, if I could get a few pain pills.

Dr. Hart said that with a punctured lung, I needed to feel the pain so if it got worse, I could come back to the ER, ASAP for treatment. He told me the ribs would heal in a few weeks, and I told him I had a few hours. He knew what I knew: with a few pain pills, I could be back on the pitch and would probably spend the night drowning in my own blood. He also described what drowning in your own blood would feel like. Like Lanny, Dr. Tom seemed wise to my ways, as well.

I had no choice but to come back to Steuber to get proper closure on my first and last real passion.

I packed my Lion's rugby home jersey for the trip but had no shorts, boots nor ball. I stopped at a sporting goods store to pick them up. The last thing was a long-needed haircut. I haven't had one since I left Chicago, and I wasn't going to go out to the pitch one last time looking like Charlie Manson. I was close to a rugby stadium, so it was easy to find a barber that knew just what I was looking for—high and tight on the sides with long, but manageable locks on top.

I was completely alone in Steuber when I stepped on the field. It was awkward at first. Unlike football, rugby is a communal game--a game of fellowship. It's very different from football and, for me, better in every respect.

Football values individual performance—you have your position assignment and do your job on every play lest you let your team down. If everyone does their specific job well, the team does well. For me, the structure was numbing. Every practice, every play, and every game is built around boundaries, assignments, and rules. You refer to your teammates by their last name in every huddle and practice. After each game, you go through the shallow ritual of slapping the hands of opponents

THE LAST LETTER

you don't know in a half-ass nod to tradition and sportsmanship as you walk off the field. You shower and go on your way.

Rugby has basic rules and halves of either 40 minutes of free-flowing action for full-side—15-players—or halves of seven minutes for seven sides—a sprinter's game with only seven players. There is a brief five-minute half-time to collect yourself. No boundaries. No time-outs, no assignments other than to act and react. You don't hide behind a face mask and pads. It's hand- to-hand combat versus the precision strikes of football. And, it's glorious.

Rugby players face each other in a line before each game, arm-in-arm. Your teammates all have nicknames. I've played with Nellie's, Jenks, Mikeys, Stenches, Shoe, Jaffa and Curls, and many, many more. When I started, I was "Magoo"—like the old cartoon character—because I couldn't see the whole field and made a lot of mistakes. That shortened to just "Goo" as I got more confident in my play and aggressive enough to "stick like goo" on an opponent—they couldn't shake me. The last three years, it morphed into "Guru", a nickname that reflected my experience, wisdom of the game, and my ability to anticipate. In rugby years I was getting old, so I guess "Guru" was better than "Moses".

After any practice or game, there was no half-ass hand shake line. There was drinking. And singing. And limericks. All of these were mixed with antics that can't be described with an R rating. You could break an opponent's nose on the field and be sliding down a beer-soaked bar floor naked laughing your asses off together two hours later. The additional bonus was that women—rugby groupies—loved it, and by the end of the party, loved me. Easy pickin's. While some weren't the best choices, the fact that there were plenty to choose from made up for it.

I had a ritual before every practice and every game and yesterday was no different. I stretched in one of the end zones, careful to smell every blade of turf with each stretch. I ripped up grass into my hands, rubbed the blades briskly, and looked to the sky to release the crushed grass and thank the rugby gods for allowing me to step into a world only ruffians and gentlemen come to know.

I spent an hour on the pitch. Running. Kicking. Punting. Chasing kicked and bouncing balls and eluding imaginary opponents on my way to the try line. The only thing missing was contact, and I do so miss the contact. I had enough grass stains but not enough stamina to go much more than that hour. It was more than I'd hoped for and allowed me to leave the pitch with no regrets. Life, especially my life, is too short for regret. There are no second chances, Larry. Treat every chance like it's the first and only one you'll ever have.

I left the ball, my cleats and socks under the center of the far goal post, walked barefoot and drenched in sweat to midfield for one last 360 view of all that I loved, then I stepped off the sacred grounds to my motorcycle. I will no longer miss the game. I will miss the camaraderie—the common bond of warriors on the field singing hideous, disgusting limericks arm in arm at the party after the match. I will miss the smell of the turf, the homage to the rugby gods. I will miss the rush of giving and taking a crushing hit. I will miss the mutual respect for the game and your opponent that only this very special game has provided to me, and those like me.

At that moment, barefoot at midfield, I was thankful for the game that gave me so much for more than a decade and gave me all of that and more in just over an hour without a single other player on the field or any mention of a Man from

THE LAST LETTER

Nantucket. It was the last sentence of the best chapter of a short life.

When I got back to the hotel I finished my laundry, pressed my shirts, and slept a few hours. My hour on the pitch really took a toll. I'm not sure if I'm that fucking out of shape, really dying that badly, nor both--but I was ass-kicked. I cleaned up, put on my freshly-pressed white Brooks Brothers French cut shirt and my Ralph Lauren jeans—the first time I'd worn either on this trip—and was ready to take my last jolt of rugby-inspired testosterone to where it could be readily applied. I was city-ready. Specifically, club-ready.

I grabbed a cab and asked the driver to take me to the hottest club he knew. I needed action. He told me he knew just where to go and that it would be around a half-hour to the Castro District and the hippest, hottest club in town, The Café. "As long as they have music and alcohol, I'm good.", I said. He told me, "Well then, a guy like you will love it!" Not long after we pulled up, I realized then that I should have also been more specific in my request and included "women."

We pulled up to The Café at around seven p.m. It was a corner bar a few stories tall with a line of about twenty dudes long waiting to get in. Yep, all fucking guys. A sausage party. A gay bar. I looked at the cabbie and just said, "Seriously?". He said, "Newest, hottest club in town, my friend." Thanks, Akmal. I gave him a damn small tip.

Now, I have no issue with gay people and have never thought of myself as homophobic. I've obviously had some experiences with mean lesbians I'd rather forget, but no issue with the fellas. I played rugby for a couple years with two gay guys—Swirvin' Irvin and Little Mark. They were the most technically sound players I'd ever played with—including

Europe--and they were both tough as nails. They had to be. Rugby is not a sport that welcomes ambiguity in masculinity.

Of course, it's easy to have no issue with minorities when you're in the majority. It's like saying "I have black friends" in Pleasantville where there hasn't been a human of African descent since the Civil fucking War. Makes you feel inclusive. Open-minded even. I had gay friends. And, black ones. Even a few Asians. I guess I'm a hell of a guy. It's all bullshit.

When you're a minority or—in my case at the Cafe—a solo in the minority, well, it's not quite as comfortable. And, looking at that line and the Freddy Mercury looking bouncer at the front of it made me consider turning right back around to drink some good Jack and Cokes at the Holiday Inn, maybe even splurge on a few extra Valium. Problem is, I was half-hour from the gay-straight Mason-Dixon line, and I actually did look pretty damn good. Well fuck it, I got in line. A club is a club.

When I got to the front, the bouncer was more like an enormous Freddy Mercury complete with the fucked up teeth. Like if Andre the Giant and Freddy had a gay kid. Tight white pants and a tight white tank top that barely covered one hell of a physique. There was going to be no messing with Freddy. Cover was $20. I don't like paying covers, and never pay $20 unless it's a damn fine strip club, which I'd hoped this wasn't. Well, fuck it, I paid the cover and walked in. A club is a club.

When I walked through the door there were two stories. The top was darker than it should have been with a balcony and tables that overlooked the lower level. The lower level was consumed primarily by a dance floor that had a Saturday Night Fever plexiglass floor with hypnotic moving neon lights underneath. There were two large bars--one an impressive floor-to-ceiling array featuring every brand of alcohol ever made, and another tap bar with what looked like an endless row of taps of every beer but Budweiser. There was a dark hallway to the bathrooms that I had no intention of stepping into that night, and past that was a better-lit room with several pool tables and a few dark corners that seemed certain to be occupied soon.

Doesn't matter if you're in the backwoods of Idaho or the gayest bar in the Castro District—always have one drink to measure up the field and the players. Always. I was a little intimidated, so I tucked myself into the corner of the bar by the entrance and asked a bartender with tuxedo pants, suspenders, and no shirt but cufflinks and a tie for a Manhattan, hold the cherry—straight-up fucking ether that only a straight man would drink at a business lunch. He asked me what kind of bitters I wanted and I got real comfortable real fast. This Chippendale wannabe knew what he was doing. There are few persons of greater value in this world than a bartender that knows what the fuck they're doing. About two sips in I realized I was going to get by just fine. It was a damn solid Manhattan.

The seven-thirty music set was pretty fucking impressive. A lot of Queen—probably a tip of the hat to Giant Freddy out front—David Bowie, Elton John, a little George Michael, and Little Richard. Shit, I could get behind this. The crowd had good energy, but nothing over the top. Took me a while to get used to seeing that many guys kiss and caress when they danced, but after my second Manhattan—which was better than the first—I had no issue.

I was an astronaut on another planet and was fine just observing without judgment, as long as the aliens didn't come at me. Weird thing is—and you know, I'm as hetero as a guy can get--these guys were all in great shape and dressed—partially and wholly—to the fucking nines.

If they were women, I'd think I'd hit the club jackpot. Like an orgy with good music and people with just enough clothes on to keep the place from being raided by the cops. Weird part is, there were no badasses. No Rusty's, Dusty's, or for God's sake, Butches. No fights. It was actually really fucking cool and the vibe was growing on me.

About midway through that second drink, a younger Asian guy named Stanley came over to me and said, "What's your name, Wallflower, and what are you doing hiding your big ass self in the corner?" No need for a "Buck McGuire" here and, actually, that may have gotten me more than I was willing to get. "Tracy", just Tracy. Perfect name for a gay bar. I mentioned to Stanley that I was straight as an arrow and just happened into the place. "A bromosexual? That's too precious." He explained that a bromosexual is a straight guy that hangs out with gay friends. I really didn't qualify, but it seemed to make him happy to meet one, so I played along.

Stanley stopped back to check on me every drink or two and brought others over to meet me like I was a lost Labrador retriever that happened into a dog show. Lots of "My God, he's adorable!", "Can I take the poor guy home?", and, "Where did you find him?" comments. I just smiled, waved, and nodded like a prince in a Disneyland parade.

In the meantime, the music got louder with a harder club beat and the lights got trippy as shit. It was like a volcano that was finally erupting. By 10, the place was packed and the dancefloor was straight- up pounding. Stanley came over and pulled out a triangular white pill with an "X" on it. Told me to take it and said it would help me dance. "I really don't want

THE LAST LETTER

to dance, Stanley, but I appreciate it.", I yelled into his ear. He responded, "You DO want to dance, you just don't know it yet." Not a bad response. And, I have to admit, except for all the dudes, the music and alcohol--like any other club--did make me want to get out on the floor.

I yelled back, "Nothing personal, Stan, but I've never been in a gang bang before and don't want to end up passed out in the bathroom of a gay bar getting fucked all night." He responded, "Relax, Shirley Temple, it's ecstasy and you definitely won't pass out, but you will have more fun than you've ever had in your horribly straight life—promise". Stanley seemed like a good-hearted guy, and I figured I'd spent the last two months choking down narcotics, free-based Vicodin, drank moonshine, and had about a half-pound of Humboldt County Randy's hybrid ganja left in my satchel, so the what-the-fucks got the best of me and I popped it in my mouth and washed it down with a smooth pina colada with a rum floater perfectly curated by the Chippendale bar tender.

Jesus. The first half-hour was tough—anxious, like I wanted to crawl out of my skin. But by 11 O'Clock, I was in the middle of the dancefloor, shirtless, soaked with sweat, and someone put a fucking karate kid headband on me for an added touch. "Cobra Kai!" It was the most energy I'd had in months like I was pure sunlight surrounded by mirrors. I was suddenly gay as fuck, except for the sex with dudes part. It was fucking awesome. I was fucking awesome. The guys were fucking awesome. The music was in-fucking-tense! I was the best bromosexual in the city for about three hours.

Maybe it was the ecstasy. I think it was more that I wasn't in the bar as a predator looking for prey. Or, maybe because there was no threat of a fight so I didn't need to keep my guard up. Actually, it wasn't that simple. I think it was the crowd. The feeling of love, freedom, and acceptance I felt from a community of people that existed in that very spot because its members were provided very little of each of those things where they came from. They live here to be accepted and loved and seem to provide that freely to strangers. One thing was for certain—I have never felt it anywhere else, and I've left more places than most people will ever go.

At around 2 a.m., the crowd was starting to thin and I was asked to go to an after-party. The "X" was starting to draw down and so was I. I grabbed a shirt from a table—trust me, there were plenty to choose from—and found Stanley, who looked to have found a companion for the night based on the spit-swapping they were doing off the side of the dance floor.

I interrupted and thanked him for being such a good guy, told him I wished I was gay enough to keep the party going, but that I was leaving early in the morning to head out of town so it was time for me to catch a cab.

He just smiled and waved me off with one hand while his other slipped down his friend's back to his ass. I knew the look, and the move, and had employed it many times myself in the past with women. He had more pressing business to tend to and was done babysitting the straight guy, the lost Labrador. I jumped in a cab and laughed nearly all the way back to the Holiday Inn and crashed hard once I got to my bed.

This morning sucks. I spent a week's worth of energy last night and today my tank is way fucking empty. I'm running on fumes. Need to get this in the mail, roll down Highway 120, and recharge in the meadows and grandeur of Yosemite which, for some reason, feels like it may be my last stop—and I'm fine with that.

My regards to Debbie and to you. Not sure if I've said it up to now, but it's worth pointing out—I appreciate being able to share this journey with someone, especially someone I trust and respect. May be best to keep my almost gay for a night thing just between us kids though. I was just gay enough for a few hours not to have either of us talk about it any further.

As Always,
Tracy

At the end of the tape, I leaned back in my chair and recalled the weekend Debbie and I spent in Chicago with the kids about five years ago. I was there for a VA conference, so we used the opportunity to experience city life for seventy-two hours or so. I had called Tracy beforehand to let him know we would be there and he did not offer to be our host as much as he demanded to show us his city, including a Sunday afternoon rugby match against a team from Cleveland.

That Saturday we went to the Lincoln Park Zoo for the kids, and the Art Institute for Debbie and me. He was obviously proud and knowledgeable about his adopted hometown, and he was funny and attentive with the kids. We had dinner that night at the Rainforest Café, which the kids loved, but left a great deal to be desired for our adult palettes. I would have thought over-priced chicken strips and tables full of families would have provided ample discomfort to a single urbanite like Tracy, but he seemed immersed in the experience like he had the opportunity to have the joy of children for a few hours without the lifelong commitment they require.

We met him early Sunday afternoon for the game at

a field in the West Loop. He was self-effacing, funny, and welcoming once he saw us. He spent a half-hour with us, then went to prepare for the game. Once he stepped onto the field we saw a different person—a person we were not at all familiar with. Once the whistle blew to start the game, he was fierce and focused.

He seemed to relish both delivering punishing hits and receiving them. Early in the game, two Cleveland players converged on him at full speed and knocked him several feet out of bounds. He immediately jumped up and clapped and sprinted onto the field. It was as if he was standing in a thunderstorm hoping for lightning to hit him so he could harness the voltage and deliver it to his opponents. And, he did deliver it.

Tracy hit one player head-to-head and split a gash just above his opponent's eyebrow that bled heavily, forcing him out of the game. Near the end of the game, he threw another player down with such force that he was knocked unconscious, I assume from a concussion.

He did not play with joy, but with a disciplined and unbridled violence we had never seen, even in bar fights I had witnessed. It was a controlled fury and it amazed me and left Debbie deeply unsettled.

After the game, in which Cleveland won, he was in the center of a ring of players leading chants thanking the other team and the referee. He was not castigating his teammates, there were no f-bombs and he was not sulking, all of which surprised me. The game and the ritual it provided for him had clearly become bigger than the outcome. He showed respect for the process I had not expected, particularly with his team on the losing end. The biggest surprise came as the players left the field.

Once he crossed the boundary line of the field, he was Tracy again. Just. Like. That. He was back to laughing and picking up the kids for a picture as if the last ninety minutes had never happened. It was bizarre.

Debbie was still shaken by what she witnessed and said, "You weren't very nice to those other guys out there." He paused, mildly confused with that same faint look into the distance he had with David on the library steps contest in college, then reached down to hold the kids and smiled and said, "It's a fun game to watch, isn't it? I sure love it". Neither of us was sure why he seemed to have some sort of cognitive dissonance to Debbie's point. It was as if he did not want to speak for the person we saw on the field, and that person certainly would not be available for further questions.

I look back at what I know now and can only think that this game provided him with license for controlled aggression that a bar fight could not. A method of exorcising demons he was not ready to acknowledge. It provided a plate to feed his hunger for validation, a hunger no other dish could successfully satisfy. That field was a bubble where some other self within him could be expressed without judgment or repercussion.

My hope in listening the second and third time to that portion of the tape was that it may have been the only place his hunger could be fully satiated until those last barefoot steps off the field in Palo Alto. My hope was that, slowly, unknowingly, he was finding peace with the many demons none of us—including Tracy--were aware that still lay within him.

CHAPTER 13

THE FEARSOME DEATH OF A STRAINED SOUL

The next few letters were postmarked from the post office at Yosemite National Park which had a distinctive postmark featuring the most prominent landmark of the park, Bridalveil Falls, with water cascading over it. It was a postmark created for postcards, I am sure, and not for the content of the letters that painted a deeper, richer, and—ultimately—darker picture of his experience there. They were letters rather than tapes, so they were much briefer

THE LAST LETTER

and in that pursuit of brevity had fewer words, each with far greater power than the more superfluous descriptions on tape.

The first letters from Yosemite were short, purposeful, and--for a reason I could only assume--less profane than any of the others I had read and listened to up to that point. It allowed for a compilation of noteworthy observations:

I finally made it! My last must-do before I die. The return to my favorite place to climb and one of the most inspiring places on the planet. To once again be reunited with the intimacy of the rock and the loose community of climbers—"Dirtbags"—that all come for the same sensation that can't be matched in any other wilderness pursuit. It's a sensation I have no business trying to describe. I'm certain you wouldn't understand it because I really don't. Dirtbags don't even try to describe it, but we all know it. We talk about how gnarly a wall was. We laugh at miscues that without a rope would clearly cost your life. The end of every night is spent around a fire with alcohol and weed recounting bold moves and sharing stories from other walls that are "must do's", even though there is no more sacred place for a climber than Yosemite.

Dirtbags are entirely different than expeditioners, just as rock climbing is entirely different from mountain climbing-- although the two are often inaccurately lumped together. I've done a good deal of both, for entirely different reasons. I've summited five of the Seven Summits, including Vinson Massif in Antarctica on a particularly harsh two-week mid-summer effort.

The planning, cost, and logistics for a major summit expedition are daunting. The planning for an epic two-day, seven- pitch climb starts when you show up. Stamina trumps technique on a summit attempt. And, scaling a face is nearly all technique. It's the difference between brick-laying and sculpting; painting a house versus painting a masterpiece.

You don't ever attempt a summit without several months of discussion and letter writing with your team. You end up knowing them better than yourself. You have to. Trust and compatibility over a week or two on a mountain is the difference between success and failure, and failure is measured in consequence, usually death.

The conversation among expeditioners is also very different than among climbers. The end of each day includes a recap of the day, changes in the plan related to weather and mountain conditions, strategies for the next day, then rest. It's all business with a few laughs and little, or often no, alcohol and definitely no recreational drugs. It's a shared misery—the price you have to pay for a ticket to the top. Five to fifteen days of focus for the reward of summiting and returning back relatively unscathed.

Climbing offers the same freedom of expression verbally as it does physically. The end of the day is filled with laughs, fucks, shits, and dammits along with whiskey, beer, tequila, reefer, and a quick five minutes on the favored route for the next day.

The commonality they share is danger, but even that is different. There are a ton of fucking things that can injure or kill you on a mountain and plenty more time for them to happen. On a wall, danger is measured per move and you can usually make it through a few hour or couple-day climb with nothing more than callused and bloody knuckles. I don't know the stats, but just about anything can kill you on a mountain. Only stupidity and overconfidence will kill you on a wall.

Fear is the common bond between the two. The reason to do both isn't to overcome your fear, but to learn how to harness

THE LAST LETTER

it to your advantage. Fear gives you adrenaline and focus, and you need both to succeed. Fear is fine as long as you know it's there, respect it, and keep it at arm's length to help you make good decisions. Once you let fear inside you, you're fucked. It consumes you and turns that adrenaline and focus against you with indecision and weakness which, in turn, leads to very bad decisions with worse consequences. My dad is an avid golfer, and in golf, they call it the "yips". Once you have it inside you there's no way to shake it.

When a person keeps fear at a distance it will reward your respect with a feeling that nothing else on this earth can provide. It's not an endorphin rush, like great sex or a crushing hit, or even a perfect pitch to a client at work. It's more. More than you can get from any drug I've tried. It's a mellow rush that lasts a long, long time and is so burned into your psyche that all you have to do is close your eyes weeks or years later and you can get it back in brief, satisfying bursts. It is that perfect feeling that you became something more than you were.

And, that is why I am here. When this all started, I figured if I died in the ocean or on a cool granite face, I'd die complete, and that will help me with whatever comes after.

The letters described a world of interesting characters with no real names and climbing routes with more interesting names yet—names like Manure Pile, and The Grack, and Apron Jam—and a very detailed description of the complex system of route ratings—the Yosemite Decimal System—that while interesting information, I doubt I would ever need to retain.

He provided details of each climb over three days that grew, according to his description of the ratings, increasingly challenging. There were vivid descriptions of each night with new friends he would meet and just as quickly forget—a vagabond community that seemed to change with each new day—as well as the descriptions of the deep shadows of the mountains against a dark sky beaming with the incandescence of a million stars.

I read the last of his Yosemite letters toward the end of my hour and wished I had not. Not because of the length, but due to the content. I thought it would be like the few before it and would be a quick, interesting glimpse into a world I had never thought to know. It clearly was not, and after I read the first paragraph I knew I would have to reset my alarm and--in this rare instance--light another Camel.

Larry,

It almost ended here yesterday, and I wish it had. I am numb. I am empty. Broken. Cancer won, Larry, and I didn't have the balls to finish both me and the cancer off for good when I had my chance. Fear begets cowardice, and fear got inside me. It claimed me. It won. I am a coward.

I connected with two dirtbags at camp Wednesday night. They planned to climb Coonyard Pinnacle, a 5-pitch 5.9 that rewards you at the top with a straight view over the canyon to Half Dome. They had the gear and I had my harness and climbing shoes. I'd had a few good days on the walls and felt ready.

I got to the top of the third pitch and was locked in on belay as Cheese and Alex were ascending. My legs were dangling off the ledge and all I could think about was jumping. My thoughts of suicide have grown in both frequency and intensity and I don't know why. Do I want to kill the cancer, even if I go with it? Am I just I'm tired of the puking blood and the fucking pain? Maybe I'm just tired. I wanted to go out on my terms, but I don't even know what the hell my terms really are, and doubt I ever knew.

The confusion is paralyzing. It's too late to see a shrink, but the urge to kill myself is so, so strong. On that ledge, I reached back to the cam to unlock my daisy chain and take the fall. Then, I thought of my family. I was such a coward to leave them without telling them. I told myself I was saving them from the pain, but I wasn't.

I was saving myself from the pain. Dying wasn't real then and that would have made it real for all of us. I was, and still am, afraid of that pain. Now numbing pain is all I feel. It's not "play through the pain" type of pain. I've never felt pain like this. Sadness. Darkness. It's a desperate pain. Like someone, something, finally told me the charade is over, but not in voices, just blank stares from faceless people surrounding me. I am not the man I thought I was. The man I tried to be. I'm empty. The pain is so fucking unbearable.

It's the pain of shame. I've never really felt pride and I've never felt much shame. They are yin and yang, like love and fear. My accomplishments—on the field, in the wild, or at work—never brought me pride. They just were. I am not really proud of anything I've done, just satisfied that I've done it. I guess it's like what Tawny, my Winnemucca masturbation coach, said is the difference between pleasure and satisfaction. Tawny may have been more savvy, more human than I gave her credit for.

I have also never really felt shame. No guilt. I've been embarrassed many times, but never ashamed of anything I've done. If what I felt on that ledge and feel at this moment is shame, it's despicable. Worse than cancer. And, I cannot shake it, even as I write. If shame is breathless, and oppressive, this must be it. I don't feel worthy of the love I've been given—even by Grandma Bea. And, I am ashamed of the love I've turned away. Jesus.

Just as I was ready to un-clip and take my fall, I heard Cheese yell up to me, "Slack in." Then I realized that if I jumped those two would be dangling on a rock face with no anchor. I would kill them, even though I was the only one that deserved to die. That wanted to die. I reached back to the rope and my belay device and slowly, painfully pulled in the slack. Just as Cheese was coming to the ledge to belay in and bring Alex up, I started vomiting. It was hard and bloody. The rock was covered in fresh blood and my mouth had that acrid iron taste. The taste of my own blood after a hard hit used to make me fight harder. This was just the taste of a slow, painful death and it poisoned my will.

Cheese said, "We have to get you down, Bro." I didn't have enough strength to take one more move up the face or rappel down. I was embarrassed. I failed myself and my partners. Cheese re-tied me and lowered me down to Alex at the base of the second pitch. It took over two hours to get all of us back down. It should have taken 30 minutes. I had no energy. Nothing.

They wanted to take me to the ranger station for help and I told them if they got me back to the campground I'd be okay. I lied and said it must have been food poisoning or bad tequila from the night before. It was the longest walk of my life. My legs could barely support me and I couldn't keep my head up to look where I was going. Cheese and Alex were steady but shaken. Like all climbers, they'd seen death and injury, but they had never witnessed injury by death. Neither had I. I wasn't wounded. I was dead. Dead inside.

At camp I took a large drink of Jack from my flask and the whiskey didn't touch it. Took 2 Valium and a Vicodin. Nothing. It was 4 p.m. and I crawled in my bag. Time stopped. Minutes felt like days, and the days were long and empty. No thirst. No hunger. No chills or sweating. I stared at the inside of my tent, and it was an abyss of orange polyester. Tears randomly dropped from my cheeks. I felt nothing, and could only hear my heart race until finally, this morning, I woke up.

I have to go back. I have to tell my family. I have to die if dying will make this emptiness stop. I cannot live with this feeling but I don't have the courage to make it stop. I am packing up and heading east. I have to go home.

Tracy

I stared at the letter and put my barely lit cigarette out. The taste of tobacco was suddenly appalling to me. Then I felt something run down my left cheek with a slow, annoying tickle. It was a tear. Then, another on the other side and within a minute, many, many more. I had not cried since my daughter was born after a difficult, strenuous delivery. Those were tears of joy and relief, but these tears were different.

I have not cried when friends or family have passed; have never cried at a sad movie or book. I could not understand where the tears came from or why they were there. I only knew they were not stopping. I then realized that the spirit of the friend that I knew had died on the rock face that day and he had to live with what little was left.

I still do not know why, but I felt his pain as if it were my own. It was devastating. There would be no more tapes; no pictures; no more high-speed chases, and no more star-covered skies. The only thing that remained was the shell of the man I once knew that was no longer alive. Cancer had killed his spirit and left his body to suffer the consequences. His very essence had become a casualty in a war he had not realized until that point that he had already lost.

His journey, and therefore mine, seemed to be at an end. I looked at the neatly sorted pile on the floor and realized there were several more letters and packages, but I had no interest in the contents. None. I collected myself, put the letter back in the envelope, and put it in its place in the order. I left the shop to return to the house with an unfamiliar void. Tracy's hope had died and my hope for a fitting end to his journey had perished with it.

I have often gone back to some of the letters and tapes to re-read or listen to them to assure I was accurately transcribing the content, including the Rapid City letter in my safe. This was the only letter that I would never open again.

I chose not to return to the shop for a few weeks. I did not want to continue going through the material and questioned whether I wanted to complete this horrible task I had been given without volunteer.

One morning over coffee in the kitchen Debbie, as wives are wont to do, asked why I hadn't been in the shop for a while. "Winter getting to you, or you just out of projects?"

I was distracted, almost annoyed, by the mild inquisition. "I have a few things, but nothing pressing. There are a few things that are too complicated to jump back into." I'd

THE LAST LETTER

hoped this modest variation of the truth would put her questions to rest. She pressed on.

"Spring isn't far away, so you better wrap them up before we get too busy with the kids.", seeming as if she were almost daring me to press on.

While she did not know what those "projects" were, I could sense that she knew I had to return to the shop and had to complete what I had started even though it seemed to have ended for me that cold February night. I would have to bring closure to my friend's journey so I could bring closure to my own.

I knew there was more. There were more letters and parcels. When I did return, I was tempted to open the final letter in the sequence, like reading the last few paragraphs of a book when you are far from the final chapters. As an avid reader and a renewed writer, I knew that would be cheating the efforts of the author, regardless of how painful those efforts may have been. I had come too far with Tracy to cheat him out of the last, labored scenes of a play that started with his last letter.

CHAPTER 14
LIFE, LOVE, AND DEATH IN DENVER

The next letter was postmarked from Grand Junction, Colorado. He had taken a northerly route out of the park, connecting with Highway 50 across the barren deserts of Central Nevada and Utah. Based on the date of the postmark, he had settled in at Grand Junction three days after he left Yosemite. There was no reference to where he had been or what had happened during those three days, leaving me to assume they were better left in the dark shadows of time.

The letter was as brief as his stopping point toward home.

Larry,

It was getting late in the day today and I had the choice of stopping in Grand Junction for the night or driving another couple hours to Glenwood Springs. My mom lives in Glenwood, and I thought about crashing for the night at her apartment, disclosing my situation, and moving on eastward to make peace with the rest of my family.

I love my mom and I know that she loves me as only a mother can love their child. But, she's a wild card. She would either tell me she knows a healer that can cure me, as any mother would offer in a desperate attempt to save her child. Or, she would insist I stay with her while she burns incense and has some shaman rub goat piss or something over my now-swollen stomach. I don't have the time or energy for any of that.

She would also tell the rest of my family whether I was still there or as soon as I'd leave- because she would want the credit for being the first in our family to have known of my situation so she could prove she had the strongest bond with me. It's a weird habit of hers, and it wouldn't be fair to the rest of my family. They must all find out at the same time and in the same way. I plan to stop in Denver tomorrow for a few days of rest in a much-needed decent hotel so I can write to each of them before I continue back to Chicago. I'll send the letters to you so you can decide if there's a need to forward them and, if so, the right time to do it.

I am exhausted, and it's not cancer. I do everything I can to fall asleep and when my eyes open I feel damned to have to face another day. My only focus is getting home, wherever that may be now.

--Tracy

A cardboard parcel postmarked from Denver was the next in the sequence. It was postmarked a few days after Grand Junction and contained five pre-addressed and stamped envelopes wrapped in a rubber band, with a separate cover letter and a dozen photographs of the mountains. It was surprisingly refreshing for me to see photos again. They were landscape photos and it renewed my hope. If he was attentive to the world around him once again, perhaps he was focused less on the decaying world within him.

Larry,

I've spent the last few days in Denver with the intent of writing to each member of my family—my parents, Katie, Tom and my aunt Jan. Jan is my closest relative of all so she deserves to know first-hand. She inherited every ounce of my grandma Bea's unconditional love, wisdom, and humility. She will understand. I know she will. I hope she will.

I'm at the Crawford Hotel in LoDo-a cool neighborhood just off downtown where there's a nice mix of sketchy fuckers and cool-vibe restaurants and bars. I decided to end this past week of isolation and needed to go back to seeing people in a place where I don't need to be seen. I need the obscurity right now.

I haven't puked blood since the ledge on Coonyard, but the pain is getting more intense and the left side of my stomach is hard as a rock. The tumor is growing and my appetite,

THE LAST LETTER

even with the last of Humboldt County Randy's super-weed, is shrinking. I eat what I can when I can. After the ledge, my appetite for everything—food, alcohol, sex, and drugs— disappeared and hadn't come back until I got to LoDo. I don't know or care why, but the hunger for each has come back in fits and spurts which is enough for me.

I know I don't have to kill myself now. This fucking thing in my body will take care of that soon enough. It's weird, but I am relieved. It's a choice I couldn't make and I'm glad it's back off the table.

I didn't want to be "that guy" that writes from the quiet loneliness of a hotel room with a bottle of Jack and a head full of doubt. If I'm going to write to the people I care about, I need to be around people. I found a cool restaurant near the Crawford and wrote to my family from there the past few afternoons before the after-work crowd fills the place. I can eat, drink and write in peace. When the crowd rolls in, I pack up and head back to the Crawford then get on my Gold Wing and drive up to a nice spot on Squaw Peak road to watch my last mountain sunsets.

Give my regards to Debbie, and hug those kids, Larry. We're about done here.

Just Me,
Tracy

The tenor of the letter was distinctly different than the "letter from the ledge". Something had happened between the arid basin of Nevada and the city lights of Denver. I do not know enough about death and dying to understand what it may have been.

That part of him that allowed him to define himself didn't die on that cliff. The desert of Nevada was his cocoon. His essence didn't dissolve as much as it may have metamorphized into something more resembling his soul—the Tracy we would all see in bits and bytes, surrounded by the bluster and façade of who he thought he should be.

I was sure he had not realized it, but there was too much evidence in that parcel to dispute it—the re-emergence of "fuck" in his vernacular, the first pictures he had sent in several days, and his letters to loved ones. All subtle clues that when put together provided me with hope, and with that hope a renewed desire to progress through the rest of the material. Without realizing it, he was re-engaging in his journey and I was therefore re-engaged in mine.

His next letter revealed what I believe to be the reason for his return, although diminished, to his pre-Yosemite self. He had found affection, and few things hold the healing power of love.

Larry,

As Zero Mostel would say, a funny thing happened on the way to the forum. Horrible movie, by the way.

The past few days I've been writing at Marg's, a small bistro with ample pours and good bad for you Mexican food. The first afternoon the manager came to my table as managers do. I looked up from my letter and saw—and I know I'll suck at describing this—but I saw the most beautiful woman I've ever seen. I've had plenty of mesmerizing eye contacts, usually as the hunter gazing at the hunted. This was different. She was different. Her eyes were warm and slightly drawn, surrounded by the most comforting face of any woman I've met. She wasn't

THE LAST LETTER

hot. She wasn't fuckable. She was, at that first glance, like home.

Her name is Tess Thompson. She has shoulder-length, curly auburn hair and a 5'8" slender, shapely body that was wrapped tightly in a floral sun dress. That would normally be enough to catch my eye, having a deep appreciation for all things slender and shapely. I barely noticed because I couldn't take my eyes off hers. The rest was just window dressing.

She introduced herself and her role and asked if I was enjoying my drink. I stumbled like a third-grader with his first crush, and barely remember what I mumbled out. I have never believed in love at first sight, and I'm definitely not falling in love before I die, but I do know a connection when I see it. This was a connection, a damn rare connection, like the universe was only the two of us circling each other. I'm certain very few people have had a connection like this and God bless those lucky ones that have.

The past few days as I've come in to write she has stopped by a few times and today she finally sat down across from me. It was 3 in the afternoon, so the place wasn't busy and we talked for twenty minutes that seemed to last a lifetime. Our eyes never left contact the entire time. Her gaze is hypnotic. It was like she was looking into my heart and I had no defense to obstruct her view. No chain link fence. No gate. I didn't have a chance.

Our eyes were telling our stories—stories of depth and darkness, joy and pain, of struggled paths that led us to that very table at that very moment—our conversation just seemed to be background noise against the dialogue of our souls. I didn't hear her words. I felt them. Trippy. Trippy as fuck, actually.

I did catch myself quickly enough to know I couldn't tell the tragedy of my truth. When she asked what I was doing in town I told her I was a freelance travel writer and was in the area for a few days working on a story. The weight of my truth made telling that lie, at that moment, seem like the smartest thing to do for both our sakes. Let's face it, my truth is a pretty horrible truth and would turn into a pretty quick buzz kill, and right now this little buzz is worth keeping alive.

Tess, it turns out, is divorced and the mother of two young kids. She's managed the restaurant for four years and I'm guessing she is around 37 or 38. And, none of that matters. I have no desire to sleep with her—I don't want to cheapen this by making the attempt. She is too good for that, and for me. She isn't a roller coaster, or an Amtrak through Kansas. Not a science project. She is quite simply what I'd always wondered that a woman could be.

I haven't ever laughed or smiled so much in a half-hour that seemed like forever. When she left the table to go back to work, I didn't want the conversation to end—a rarity for me. Forever never lasts as long as we'd like or want. I needed to quit while I was ahead.

Once she left, I was suddenly famished. My hunger was back. Hard. I ate two entrees, drank three more margaritas, and came back to the hotel. I plan to spend a few more days than I'd planned in Denver. More later.

Your Travel Writer Friend,
Tracy

Love is often not convenient and it is usually more obvious to observers than those stricken with it. I could tell he was in love and I was initially very happy to read about it, particularly since a genuine love—a love not complicated by sex or circumstance—had seemed to have eluded him most of his life.

However, love has consequences and is occasionally not kind. I grew concerned whether he would allow love to flourish so near to his own demise or if he would choose a wiser, less painful path for them both and leave love on the table at a trendy urban restaurant after that first half-hour. Love left in the moment, in this case, would be better than love left to loss.

When I returned to the house, the sudden and positive development was reflected in my mood. I was also laughing and smiling more than I had all winter. Debbie was watching television with the kids and I sat next to her on the couch, wrapped my arms around her, and whispered, "I love you" in her ear.

She smiled and turned to me and said, "What's gotten into you?" as the kids starred at the television and scribbled in coloring books on the floor.

"Just happy to see winter finally fading." was the only response I could think of, and it seemed to satisfy her curiosity. A hug with deep affection behind it combined with a tender affirmation of love tends to quell all questions.

After a week—seven letters and a package of photos, several including his newfound love—he sent a long letter that was perfectly typed and printed from a computer.

Dear Larry,

I can type faster than I can write and Tess let me borrow the computer in her office, so here I sit for an hour that she's working on the floor, with a shaker full of tequila sunrise--the brunch of champions.

Yesterday, I met Tess's boss, Shiloh Gates. What a fucking character. She brought him over to my table and introduced us.

"Tracy McGuire, meet Shiloh Gates, the owner of Marg's."

I stood up to shake his hand and said, "Is that Shiloh, like in the Bible, or Shiloh like the church where the rebels got their asses kicked in the Civil War?"

He shook his head and without pausing said, "Did your parents name you Tracy so you'd get your ass kicked like a 'Boy Named Sue', or were they just hopin' you'd bring home a nice boyfriend?"

We both gave each other the smirk and nod members of the smartass club are wont to do. Shiloh and I were going to get along just fine. He had Tess bring us a few shots of premium tequila and we sat down. He is every bit the wise-ass as I am, but older, smoother, and way more savvy than my simple self.

Shiloh's back story is interesting. He actually was born near that Civil War battlefield, hence the name, and moved to Beaumont, Texas when he was young. After graduation from the University of Texas, he was an undercover agent for the FBI for 8 or 9 years, settling in Denver where he made connections with both local law enforcement and the criminals they were trying to catch. He was shot in the side during a sting—showed me the scar; it was impressive—and left the Bureau to open a restaurant. He parlayed his connections to open more restaurants and now owns six in the metro Denver area, including Marg's.

I had a good and honest lie going with Tess regarding my travel writing career, and he quizzed me on that. He's a good interrogator, asking questions nonchalantly like he's just trying to keep the conversation going while getting all the information he needs for when he needs it most, always throwing out bait to catch a lie.

"What magazines had my work been in?" "Where was my favorite place?" "What was I writing about in Colorado... maybe he could help."

I answered well enough to put him at ease and legitimize my purpose. I could tell he liked the thought that his restaurants may get included in my work—I had possible value and enough value at that moment for another shot of some of the best tequila I've ever sipped.

He asked me to go with him to a few of his other restaurants to check-in, so we got into his Cadillac—with personalized "SHILOH" license plates, and a Texas-shaped key tag with a large silver bullet and a dozen keys on the ring. We drove to three of his other joints, stopping for a drink and conversation with the manager at each. The restaurants were all different but they shared one thing in common—younger, attractive female managers that all spoke to Shiloh in a weirdly boyfriend-girlfriend tone, and that never let his tall Texan glass of that moment's mixed drink of choice draw down very far. Impressive.

When we got in the car, I joked with him that he didn't seem to have restaurants as much as a harem of damn hot women running them. He turned serious for the first time that afternoon and said, "They're all damn good at what they do. They're all single, so have at it if you'd like. Just don't ever touch Tess." It wasn't a statement as much as a threat.

"You and Tess have something going on, Shiloh? Because if you do, I have no intention of getting in the middle of that."

"Fuck no!" he said as we drove off. "I'm happily married and that's the way I plan to keep it. She's just different than the others. Just better."

There is obviously something going on there, but it's not my business and I don't plan to stay in town, or alive for that matter, long enough to find out. Plus, he was right—she did seem better than the others, but in what way I really don't know. She just is.

Our last stop was a strip club. We walked right past the bouncer, paid no cover, and we were escorted to a private room. Yep, Shiloh and I are going to become fast friends. It has been a while since I'd seen a naked woman, and I forgot how good a stripper that knows her trade can make you feel. They make you feel mighty fucking good. One started to unbutton my shirt and I stopped her before she could see the growing lump on my left side. Even a stripper isn't paid enough to see that. Shiloh looked over and said, "What's the problem, Buddy? You shy?".

I shot back and said, "I'm paying to see them naked. If I undress, I'd have to charge them double."

It worked in Winnemucca, and Denver was no different. The four girls in the room laughed and Shiloh did, too. I settled for a very thorough lap dance. Shiloh left the room with two of them for around twenty minutes and came back and said it was time to go.

On the way back to the Crawford, Shiloh told me if there was anything I needed, let him know. I had no doubt he could come through. While he's not the most attractive guy—thinning hair on top with a curly blond mane in back, a little like Dwight Yoakam, complete with the snakeskin boots—he is a charming mother-fucker. And, everywhere we went he got what he wanted from who he wanted it from. He was smooth, like my old boss, Rex, but with better connections and what seemed like a murkier past.

Just as we pulled up to the hotel he opened his glove

compartment to reveal a shiny, black .38 Special revolver. He said, "If the shit ever gets real, don't hesitate to reach for 'Sunshine' here. It's unmarked, so no trace and no trouble."

I asked why he'd name a gun.

"All my guns have names. Sunshine here is so named so you can stick it where the sun don't shine. It's loaded, so just be careful. If you grab for it, there better be a damn good reason."

I've met people like Shiloh before. They're favor brokers. You want weed? Shiloh doesn't smoke, but he knows where to send you. Coke? Same thing. Women? Sure enough. At the end of any transaction, you and the supplier both owe a little something to Shiloh. Need a new car? Shiloh's buddy—and everyone's a "Buddy"—will give you a great deal…and owe Shiloh. People like Shiloh treat connections like capital, and life's purpose is to obtain as much capital as possible and keep other people from obtaining yours. It's a talent few have and I admire it. Besides, I have nothing of value to trade and no time to trade it so my value to him may have ended after he dropped me off at the hotel. We'll see.

Time's up so I better get back to my table to spend a little time with Tess before the dinner crowd comes in.

Best regards to you and Debbie!

Tracy

A few days later Tracy sent another letter with several photos. It confirmed what I had suspected regarding his feelings for Tess Thompson, and also confirmed my doubt that he would ultimately return to Chicago, or that he would exercise his better judgment based on his circumstance and tread a light path on love as his ultimate end drew closer each day.

Larry,

It's been a very good week as you can see from the pictures of the mountains and of Tess. Both are stunning. The views of each change with every ray of light. Both make me happy and help me forget the situation I'm in. The combination of the 2, of such natural and human beauty, has led to something I don't think I've felt since before I was diagnosed. Contentedness. I am damn content.

Tess doesn't work on Thursdays so I convinced her to ride into the mountains with me for the day. She was hesitant at first so I reinforced we'd be riding as friends and that I had nothing but good intentions. I was, in fact, lying. I'm not a fan of any relationship built on lies, but if this would turn into a relationship, it would be worth the exception.

It was honestly the best day I have ever spent with a woman. After a few hours of mountain riding with her arms alternating from wrapped tightly around my waist to slung over my shoulders, we stopped at a pullout beside the Snake River for a quick lunch. We were both mesmerized by of the power of the river thundering down the canyon as the breeze wisped through the pines around us in a rolling howl. If I was with any woman, it would have been a good day. With Tess, it was pure fucking magic. I wasn't going to fuck it up trying to get laid, which would be my standard operating procedure in such an orgasm-inviting setting.

After we ate, I told her I had a long-time tradition of dunking my head, and usually my whole body, in a mountain stream whenever I had the chance. It's a huge rush, like diving into the cold rolling waves of the Pacific. I went first. Like every time I've done it, the lightning bolt of ice-cold water numbed my skull and shot through my body. When I emerged I let out a deep, long growl of exhilaration. She was tentative, but followed, and screamed as her head came out of the water. Her face came alive with a smile and a glance that melted me. I ran my fingers through her thick, wet auburn hair and welcomed her to being one with a greater nature than she previously knew.

She asked what a full-body dip was like.

"Better. Much better." I said.

She provided a seductive, inviting smile, never took her gaze off of my eyes, and started to undress. I followed without concern for what she might think about the bulging tumor on the left side of my torso, never taking my eyes off hers. She got down to her underwear and stopped. I didn't. She grabbed my hand, took a deep breath and we both slid down a small rock into an eddy and took the plunge.

It was insanely exhilarating and numbingly cold. I'd done this plunge hundreds of times before in mountain streams in many places, but this was different. Submerging into the snow-fed waters of the Snake while holding her hand felt like I was baptizing the Virgin Mary. A simple act of pureness with the purest soul I've ever met.

The freezing cold mountain water took our breath away and when we came up we were laughing and screaming. I held her and told her to stay with me for one full minute to get the most out of the rush. It's the submersion secret. She understood the secret—she looked like she wasn't cold at all. She put her hands on my face and said, "The rush will last forever as long as I'm with you." Jesus. My mind went blank. I was hers and she was mine.

After a long, slow, beautiful kiss, I pulled her to the bank and wrapped our picnic blanket around us so we could sit in the afternoon sun to warm up and dry off.

With drops of cold water still dripping from her hair, she leaned over and whispered, "That was incredible.", and softly kissed my cheek. What I felt wasn't the tingle, Larry, it was an explosion of a thousand tingles that started at my cheek and raced across my skin then through my entire body. It was better than any orgasm. Better than a hundred orgasms. I have never felt more alive in my life, never felt more loved, and never felt more in love.

We both stared into each other's eyes as if the beat of our hearts were the only thing left in the world. She said, "I do too." Goddammit, she finished a sentence I never started. She knew exactly what I was thinking and what I was feeling and felt it, too. I was going to tell her I loved her but didn't need to. She knew it. We were talking without speaking. We were one soul, bonded with that one small kiss on the bristly whiskers of my right cheek.

Then, after what seemed like an eternity of pure light, reality hit. She asked about the large lump on my torso. There is a difference between lying and not telling the truth, and I chose the latter. I told her I had a benign growth and that after I was done with my writing here I was going to have it removed back in Chicago.

"Nothing to worry about. It looks worse than it really is." There's no way I was going to fuck up pure love with the sour taste of sympathy.

It was my turn.

"What's up with you and Shiloh?" I asked.

She was indignant. "What do you mean, 'me and Shiloh'?"

I told her, "It just seems like you two have a thing."

She became adamant, "I've never, ever slept with Shiloh Gates, and I never will."

I softly asked, "Ever thought about it?".

Her reply was filled with angst, "God no! Now, stop talking about it."

The magical moment was over, and we were both to blame. We both asked honest questions, we both gave only slight variations of truthful answers, and we both knew that once some questions are answered—truthfully or not—they should never be asked again. "It never hurts to ask.", is bullshit. It usually hurts to ask when there is no good answer to the question.

As if she were apologizing for her outburst, she pulled me close and handed me her clothes. I have undressed busloads of women in my life, but have never dressed a woman, and never thought of doing so with such a beautiful woman. It was the most gentle, romantic thing I have ever done, or been offered to do.

I kissed and caressed her legs as I reached down to put her feet in her jeans to pull them up. They were soft and supple. I knelt in front of her to button her pants, and gently kissed her bare stomach. I stood up and moved behind her to put on her blouse. Before I put her blouse on, I ran my fingers slowly across her back, over her neck, and around her bra line. She exploded in goosebumps, and I immediately followed. Button by slow button, I finished putting her blouse on, like I was robing a queen.

It was her turn. She was slow and deliberate. I had my hands wrapped in her hair, and my body took direction from her every move. She put one leg into my jeans, looked dreamily into my eyes, then kissed my chest. She put the other leg in, buttoned the jeans then pulled me against her for a deep, deep hug. She was the only thing in my world at that moment. Then, she put my shirt over my head and shoulders and grabbed the front collar to pull me to her lips for the slowest, deepest kiss I've ever had. It honestly made me light-headed, and I think my eyes rolled back in my head when we were done. I gasped. She literally took my fucking breath away. Surreal.

We walked to the bike, and I softly put my helmet over her still-wet hair. I kissed the face shield of the helmet and rubbed my forehead against it. She may never be mine, but she cast a spell over me on the banks of a roaring mountain stream, and I was happy to be enchanted.

We rode back to Denver and I dropped her off outside the restaurant. It was too public for another kiss, so she handed my helmet to me and whispered, "It was for me, too."

I was going to tell her that it was the best day of my life, but she responded—AGAIN—before I could even say it. I don't understand how that works—the connection--and I don't care to understand it. I just want more, knowing that more in my situation may be measured in days and not months or even weeks.

Before she walked away she said very firmly, "Don't ever let Shiloh know about this. Shiloh hurts people, Tracy, and he hurts people that get close to me even more."

"I'm not afraid of Shiloh Gates.", I yelled as she walked away.

She stopped, turned around, and paced toward me with her eyes now piercing, "That's because you don't know him."

The eyes that drew me with the truth of pure love were now equally as honest with deep fear. It was fear for me as much as for herself. I have never had a woman that wanted to protect me. I've always tried to protect them against the harm I might create for them with heartbreak. It was my heart she didn't want to be broken, not realizing it was already way too late for that. We both kept a secret of heartbreak from the other. I'm sure of it. I am content to accept it.

I've kept a low profile the past few days. A few hours at Marg's each day to try to catch afternoon time with Tess. Solo rides into the foothills for the sunset. I also went to dinner the other night with Shiloh and his attractive but painfully bitchy trophy wife, Cindy. They invited me to the Aspen Wine Festival this coming weekend. Told me it would make a good story for my travel article. I reluctantly agreed to go. I'm not thrilled with Cindy, but time spent with a fellow Mo-Fo like Shiloh will be damn fun time to spend. We're enough alike that it's anyone's guess what the hell kind of trouble we'll get into, and that he'll be able to get us out of.

I also used my time these past few days to call Glasgow's office. I'm down to about two scripts of pain and nausea meds and need another pad. I didn't talk to him, but his office called me back and said they'd send them to the hotel and that he mentioned that if I need more, just to call. I think both Glasgow and I know I won't be calling again.

I realize I should leave Tess before my condition gets worse. I'm not an idiot. I'm selfish, but not that fucking selfish. I am convinced that if there is a God, he introduced us for a reason. One I'll probably never know. And, if there isn't a God, a few more days of joy for a dying man won't kill anyone. If this is my first and probably best chance to touch and feel true love, I think God will be cool with me taking that chance.

LARRY REYNOLDS

God is good, Larry. If God is love, then God is good.

Just Me,
Tracy

Before I left the shop, I was thumbing through the postmarks on the remaining packages and ran my index finger across the dates and places I'd pinned on the map. Tracy's Denver days were coming to an end, but so was my hour. I was enjoying his first true love and wanted to continue to see where it ultimately took him, but not at the expense of my own family. I was starting to get rushed to finish the sessions in the shop as the days were getting longer and nights in the shop would soon be at a premium with warmer weather approaching.

I quickly put out my cigarette and decided to open one more letter in the order. It was a quick letter describing a strange turn of events. Shiloh Gates' wife, Cindy, had not accompanied them on the trip to Aspen, but a few of Shiloh's friends did—"The Yuppie Posse", as Tracy referred to them.

After a few paragraphs describing what amounted to "big men on campus" chicanery amongst the Gates Posse, Tracy noted that he returned to his hotel room early and heard a knock on the door around eleven. There was a very young and very naked woman passed out on the floor outside his door. He brought her into his room and called Shiloh, who was laughing at him over the phone, offering a simple yet appalling solution.

"You have a hot, naked lady in your room, and you're asking for my advice? Buddy, are you queer or something?

THE LAST LETTER

I happen to know where her clothes are and I'll drop them by tomorrow morning, but you'll only get them if I know you did what any man ought to do."

Thankfully, Tracy slept on the floor and explained to a very frightened young woman when she woke up that he found her and had tracked down her clothes, which were on their way to the room. On the way back to Denver, Shiloh mentioned they had drugged the woman at the bar and taken her to his room to see "what kind of man he was".

Tracy was angered by the act.

Shiloh Gates responded, "That's just in case you ever want to tell Cindy about what I do with my spare time. Everything stays between us, Buddy. Everything."

Tracy noted that he feared that Shiloh would tell Tess. Once they arrived in Denver, he was quick to disclose the incident to her in detail. Her response was simply, "That's a very Shiloh thing to do. I understand. You don't have to explain these things to me, but I'm glad you did." which seemed like a near-spousal response.

I was re-playing the incident as I walked back into the house. I realized between finding his light of love with Tess Thompson and dancing with the darker shadow of Shiloh Gates, Tracy's days in Denver may soon come to a difficult end. I worried for a moment about what may be next, then turned to the much more pressing worry of returning to the house and my family for dinner. Denver would have to wait.

I returned to the shop on a Saturday afternoon. The spring thaw was in full swing. The days-- and the optimism--grow as the cold, dark grip of winter loosens with the thaw. Soon, I wouldn't be able to return to the shop as often as family activity picks up, and I would no longer be able to take clandestine trips without the added risk of exposure longer days provide. The stack of letters was winding down along with my availability so I felt I could move through quickly as the snow slowly melted outside and the crocus waited to mark the beginning of spring.

I locked the door to the shop to assure I wouldn't be surprised by Debbie or the kids with the broader expanse of daylight then dove into the letters. Tracy had stayed in Denver three more weeks spending an increasing amount of time with Tess both at Marg's and on motorcycle trips deeper into the mountains. He had also spent more time with Shiloh Gates when he would come in for his weekly Wednesday visits to the restaurant, as well as on the weekends with his many associates of, by Tracy's descriptions, suspect character.

In one particular letter, he described a heated discussion with Shiloh at a large party at the Gates home, which seemed to mark a turning point in the relationship.

Larry,

I'm still pissed off writing this but have to get it off my chest. A friend is a friend, and I'm as loyal to a friend as you can get, but Shiloh crossed a line tonight that has me re-thinking our friendship and how the hell to bow out of it gracefully. Larry, he broke the Bro Code. And, he breaks it often and for all the wrong reasons.

I have never been confined to the same set of morals for which most people abide. I've always joked that I only have three morals: Never dance with fat chicks. Never lie to a woman unless it's for sex. And, I keep that third one variable for when

THE LAST LETTER

the situation presents it. While my three morals have always been more of a joke, there has been one actual moral code I have held above all others—the Bro Code.

The Bro Code dictates that you never hit on a bro's woman. And, if they hit on you, you never—EVER—sleep with them. You just don't. No woman is worth a friendship. The Bro Code extends to exes, too. You never hook up with a Bro's ex unless you ask for and receive express permission to do so. I have lived by the Bro Code and expected any true friend to live by it. If they didn't, the friendship is over. Done.

Shiloh shit on the Bro Code tonight. I was at a party with about 30 people at his house. Most were couples that were either upper-crusters, or wannabe upper-crusters. Not usually my scene, but he does have a hell of a nice place, and really does a party right. Shiloh and I were having a good cigar and tequila alone on his deck—incredible view of the foothills with a big ass fire pit right in the middle—and I was commenting on some of the trophy wives and asking for the back stories on the couples.

Shiloh pointed out one by one the wives and girlfriends he'd either recently, or—in a couple of cases—frequently fucked. What the total fuck?!

I asked him how and why and he just said, "They want it, and I have it. What more do you need?"

Fuck that. I asked him if he knew what the Bro Code was and if he knew that he was violating it a thousand ways. The more details he gave on each one, the more pissed off I got.

He told me, "Relax, Buddy. Look, they're the ones comin' at me. I'm not going to walk away from a good piece of ass."

I reminded him that he could get a good piece of ass walking across the street. He's a charming mother fucker. Why would he have to pick a friend's girl or, worse yet, wife. I finally asked if he'd do my girlfriend.

He stopped, put out his cigar, and said, "If your girlfriend came on to me, probably. What you ought to think about is picking a girlfriend that won't do shit like that. Don't pin this on me—it's the women."

I sat back and had an "oh-fuck" moment. While I've never—ever—violated the bro code, I had often used his same rationale for sleeping with women that came on to me. Based on the math, I'm sure plenty of them had boyfriends or even husbands, even if I didn't know the poor bastards. I had little room to judge, so just ended it with a "Whatever, dude." and the closest thing to a make-up man-hug as men can get—a tap of his glass and slamming the rest of our tequila.

I don't have a wife. I won't have a wife. I really don't even have a girlfriend. Just someone I am in love with. He's got nothing on me, nothing to take. Doesn't matter. He'd take it if he had the opportunity, and that's an opportunity I'm never going to give him.

Tough Night.
Tracy

Reading the letters, I found myself growing increasingly wary of Shiloh Gates, wondering why my otherwise savvy friend had not, and trying to better understand Tracy's insistence on staying in a relationship he would never live to fulfill and a friendship wrought with consequence. At the end of one of the letters, I tossed it on the table, grabbed my Camel between my thumb and forefinger, took a long drag, and said out loud, "Why the hell aren't you leaving? For

God's sake, get the hell out of Denver." His choices and his extended stay in a place he should have long since left were frustrating me. This wasn't the life, or the end, I had hoped to chronicle. The next letter did little to settle my angst.

Dear Larry,

I spent the most incredible night of my life last night and am lost in wonder this morning. I was at Marg's until around 7. It was later than usual, but I've spent more of each day "finishing my story" for my fictional travel magazine so I could spend more time with Tess while she worked, with an occasional late night of good tequila if Shiloh shows up. I smoked some Randy-weed to help me sleep when I got back to my room and was in bed by 9. Around midnight I heard a knock on my door. It was Tess. She closed Marg's and came to my room with a bottle of very good red wine. I paused with the door open not knowing how I could say what I wanted to say—that I loved her, that she was my person, that I was dying, and that I wanted her to be the last thing I saw before I did. Instead, I just froze as we awkwardly stared at each other.

Her eyes softened. "It's time.", she said in a near whisper.

Without saying a word, I drew her in and opened the wine, and poured each of us a glass. We sat on the bed and I simply and quietly said, "I love you." Three words I have rarely spoken--and meant even less often--to a woman. Three words that seemed shallow in describing the depth of my feelings for her.

I explained to her that it was time for the truth, and she needed to know that I was very sick and that "It's time." may not be the experience she would want it to be. She set our wine on the nightstand, turned on the clock radio, and—no shit--Phil Collins, "In The Air Tonight" was playing. A destiny song. It was, and still is, surreal.

She bent down and held my head in both her hands and kissed me first on the forehead, then the cheek, then the lips in the most slow, gentle, and deep kiss in the history of kisses. We were breathing each other's breath, caressing each other's lips and tongues like a slow dance to eternity.

She gently pushed me back onto the bed, looked close and deep into my fearful eyes, and said, "I want to make love to you, and with you, and whatever you have to give is all that I want and all that I need."

Jesus. You can put that on my tombstone. I will be able to recite that with my last breath.

She pulled off my shirt and shorts, then slowly started to kiss me from my shoulders to my toes. Each kiss perfectly timed and perfectly placed, like the warm glow of a firefly was landing every time her lips pressed against my skin and radiating through my body. It was CPR for my wounded heart.

I unzipped her dress and began to kiss every exposed inch as I went, slowly at first, then with each kiss on her supple skin more rapidly and more intense. By the time I pulled her dress and panties off, I was biting and sucking like I was on death row and it was my last meal.

The next half hour is difficult to describe because I have too much respect for her to share the details of the most intimate experience of my life. Another first for me. It will be better remembered between Tess and me if I don't share the details with others—even with you.

I will say that we were in constant motion, never apart, stopping only to look into each other's eyes before continuing. With each gaze, the intensity of our passion only grew. I was lost

THE LAST LETTER

in sea of love and a shore of flesh; afraid, as if I was diving off a high dive into a pool of pure emotion that had no bottom or sides. I whimpered at a few points—another first--and gasped in complete pleasure several times. I was completely vulnerable. My fence had crumbled and the view was incredible. I was staring into space and landscape I'd never seen before and the view was vast and never-ending.

At one point, she grabbed my palm and placed it against her heart. It wasn't beating, it was pounding a slow, hard throb as if it was going to either jump out of her skin or pull me into her soul. I pulled her hand to my chest and our hearts were beating together. Literally—the same pace, the same intensity. I'm not sure how many orgasms we had because it was all an orgasm, but better. Longer. More intense. I don't even recall if I had an erection or if I had ten. It was simply a blur of bliss and bond. Pure emotion. Pure love. Nothing like it—ever.

We finally paused and didn't speak for nearly an hour. We held each other tightly, kissed gently, and expressed every ounce of love we had for each other through the warmth of our eyes and the fire of our flesh. We were one. We were the same soul in two different bodies that, at that moment, would never be separated. I wasn't dying, I was living, and life was incredible.

I have been running from dark storm clouds since Chicago, realizing they get closer each day. I realize that the dark clouds of death will surround me sooner than later, and lightning will finally strike and kill me. Right now I look into those dark, thunderous clouds and all I see is the warm, radiating light of the sun. Tess is my sun. She is my energy and my life. The clouds are just faint shadows cast against her radiant light.

Before she left she asked me to come to her house today and meet her family. I am nervous to take a step that bold blindfolded, knowing full well I have few steps left to take. The fact that she knows my truth and my consequence and is still willing to invite me into her world comforts me. I want to know all of her. I know that I will not be disappointed and that I am committed to not disappointing her.

Wow. Just Wow,
Tracy

I continued to try to justify what could have led to Tracy's "love at first sight" experience, and why he continued to pursue it, but I could not. I have never believed in love at first sight. Love is enduring, and infatuation is fleeting. This was clearly not a love that would endure, so why was he falling so deeply, so quickly?

Was he unconsciously trying to fill one last hole, one last check off his bucket list—a true and real love—and Tess Thompson just happened to be there at the time? Yet, if I knew which breath was my last, wouldn't it be the deepest breath I would take? If this was his last opportunity for love before death, it would make sense it would be his deepest love of all. There seemed to be little sense in any of this.

Old vines or new vines, twisted vines or true vines, all will flourish with ample rain and sun. But only those vines with deep, complex roots cultivated over the floods and drought of many seasons can endure. It is that depth tested over time that allows love to survive. My love for Debbie wasn't instant, and it wasn't infatuation. I am quite certain that raising a family, struggling through adversity, and celebrating the quiet moments over time have created a love that will not be broken and will survive long after "until death do us part".

I came to realize that the end result of his love and mine was similar and that the path is of less importance than the destination. While I am concerned about what led to my friend's falling in love so deeply and so quickly, I was pleased that he had found something that had eluded him for so long. Whether he purposely avoided deep love for so long for so many reasons didn't matter. He had arrived at a very special place, and he had found the right person to share that place with. It is, and will always be, the mystery of love.

His next letters, written over a couple of weeks, described a love that went far beyond a late-night hotel room rendezvous. He did meet Tess's family. She has two young children that he quickly adored, and she lived very close to her parents and a sister and her family that quickly welcomed him.

I still found myself anxiously wondering why he would put both Tess and her family through a relationship with a sure and approaching end. It seemed selfish. Holding a lover and embracing her family are two very different things, with far greater consequences than individual love. I was disappointed and as with much of his journey found myself with more questions than he was able or willing to answer.

I kept reading as the afternoon light lowered and closed one of my last sessions with a turn of events that shifted my thoughts from the mystery of love to the ultimate and tragic end I had feared for my friend in the Mile High city.

Dear Larry,
Big Head Todd and the Monsters were right—life is

bittersweet, a combination of bitter and sweet; sweet and bitter. I have had the most incredible few weeks with Tess and her family. And, then the end. The tragic fucking end. The end that has led me to the most resolute course of action I have had since I told Dr. Glasgow about "Plan B". Like "Plan B", this is my plan and I am as convinced as any decision I've made that it's the right plan.

After a great afternoon BBQ with her family, Tess and I took a walk through a local park. We stopped by the bank of a small creek and she started weeping. She grabbed my hand and looked at me with eyes I hadn't yet seen. Painful eyes. Fearful eyes. Eyes of shame. She explained to me that while she had never slept with Shiloh Gates, he had been forcing her to provide him with oral sex when he would make his Wednesday visits for their "closed-door" meetings in her office at Marg's.

I was shocked. Dumbfounded. I've spent a lifetime providing glib responses, but I had nothing to say. My mouth was dry. My world had changed. I was shocked and finally said, "How can he force you?" It seemed impossible to me. Shiloh has enough charm that force or coercion wouldn't seem to be a necessary part of his repertoire. I was angry, but angry at her, which made me even more dizzy. The angrier I got, the more she sobbed. She went on.

He had been doing this for the better part of a couple of years and told her that it was the price she had to pay for her very nice compensation and management of the restaurant. As a divorcee with two young children, she had little choice. She claimed the managers of his other restaurants were in similar situations and held to similar tasks, and that the consequences of refusal were often harsh.

Shiloh had connections and would assure they would never

get a similar job in Denver again, or worse. Going to the cops wasn't an option—he was an ex-cop, the worst kind, and he knew enough crooked cops to make any complaint get lost.

She's considered moving her family, but felt no matter how far away she would go it wouldn't be far enough for his reach. She could never leave her parents and sister. She said far worse things happened to men, like me, that received affection from any of the women under Shiloh's watch. She begged me to leave before something horrible happened to me. As she sobbed, she just kept repeating, "He knows." Her fear—both for herself and for me—was visceral.

I realize I have been naïve. This was more than a violation of the "Bro Code". This was pre-meditated assault, at best, and rape at worst. What I had observed the past several weeks always seemed like flirtatious banter with women he'd put in positions of power. In reality, he pre-selected them for their powerlessness. The Wednesday closed-door meetings at Marg's and the comments he made about Tess and I were evidence not of a "favor broker", but an "owner of people", and those types don't take well to trespassers stepping onto their property.

At first, I was angry that she would allow it to happen. Then I was disgusted by the whole situation. I was confused. He was my friend. She was my lover. He had already taken something before it was mine. I told her I would talk to him and she begged me not to do it. He was too powerful and we would all be harmed. I held her in my arms while she cried and realized I would have to act. I eventually tenderly kissed her hand and whispered that we should go back to her house. I told her I would figure it out, but I knew I already had.

I rode back to the hotel, emptied my flask into a glass, crushed a Vicodin, and snorted half of it to see if my "figure it out" was really the best plan. It is. I have to kill my friend Shiloh Gates.

Wish Me Luck,
Tracy

It was the first time in the dozens of letters I read that I started having an animated dialogue, pacing in my shop, with my dead friend. I implored him to walk away.

"Get out of town. Get the fuck out of town! Right now!", which I believe is the first time I've ever verbalized the f-bomb in my life.

"For God's sake, do NOT carry through with your plan! No life is worth taking another."

Then I realized that no phone call, no return letter, and no personal plea would change the outcome. There would be no notifying the authorities for a deed to be done in the past. I felt powerless realizing the outcome would be in the next letters and I had no choice but to read on. Based on the content of the next letter, this would be Tracy's last Sunday in Denver and the last few minutes for me for the evening. I read on in shock in my shop.

Larry,

My plan is set and my time is short. It's a simple plan hatched with the potent clarity of narcotics and alcohol. "The devil is in the details" as old man Maxwell used to say at the agency. Well, I'm the devil, and here are the details...

I'll ask Shiloh for a ride to the bus station. Tell him I'm heading to Telluride to meet my editor because I can't trust the weather in the mountains this time of year on my bike. Telluride is far enough that he won't want to take the time to drive me, but close enough that a bus makes sense versus a plane. I'll ask to stop by the Diamond Cabaret strip club, one of his favorites, for an hour or two. It's a short hike to the bus station from there, so the Diamond is where he will die.

The killing part came to me after I snorted my Vicodin. Easy-peasy. Thank you Humboldt County Randy—your moonshining wisdom has come in handy more than once. I'll cook a half a dozen Vicodin and put the serum in my flask with some tequila. As long as he takes the first drink, it should be quick. I'll bust it over to the bus station and get the hell out of here. No trace. No witnesses. No killer. Just a bad man OD-ing in a strip club parking lot. Open and shut for the cops. Freedom for Tess and the others. And, a shitpile of money left for Cindy, which may finally put an earnest smile on her face.

My dilemma is Tess. How do I explain to her that I don't want to leave her, but love her so much that I have to go so she can be free? I can't even explain it to me. The sacrifice is so clear in my heart but makes little sense in my mind. The only way I've reconciled it is that my love for her is forever, whether I die in Denver or not. I'm willing to take this bullet so she can live a better life because the thought of her continuing this struggle after I am gone is not one I can bear.

If I get caught, I'll die in jail. So what. If Shiloh and "Sunshine" kill me—the net result is all the same. Janis Joplin was right, "When you got nothin', you got nothin' left to lose."

I can't tell Tess. Not yet. She'll know the truth soon enough, whether my plan works or not. And it better fucking work. Weirdest thing—I didn't have the courage to end my own life, but I have no doubt I can end another. No. Fucking. Doubt.

Time to get to work.

Tracy

I read the letter and hoped it was all a lie--a fantasy to save a fair maiden. I leaned back in my chair and closed my eyes hoping the next letter would detail a more reasonable escape, one without murder, arrest, and heartbreak. Or, a plan foiled by conscience and the decency to let other lives be lived regardless of the outcome.

I couldn't stop. I could not go back to my family--to my "real life"--to live with the anticipation of what may happen next. I reset my alarm, put out my cigarette, and pressed on.

The next letter was postmarked from Trinidad, Colorado. I tapped it against the desk several times wondering if I should even open it. I was anxious. Nervous. I finally opened it as if in slow motion to confirm whether my hope that he had walk away without harm would be realized. It wasn't and it was revealed immediately.

Larry,

I was packed and ready. I'd written a note to Tess that I planned to drop off in her office early in the morning before she got to work. I included several of our pictures together and the key to my motorcycle. I called Franey at the bank and gave him the dealer's name in Arlington Heights and my balance due. He's going to send a check and send the title to Tess. It will be the last best thing I can give her.

In my note to her, I told her where it was parked and to do with it as she pleased. My bike is my last prized possession. It delivered me here, to her, and it is here I want the last thing I value to stay. I told her she was the greatest lover of many and the only love I'd ever wanted. All painfully true.

Honestly, I almost didn't go through with it. I woke up at 5 a.m. and laid in bed in a dark, empty room filled with doubt. I spent an hour running through the plan, trying to get the courage to put my feet on the floor and start in motion the events and ultimate execution of my friend Shiloh Gates. I had a paralytic feeling of fear in my stomach. Not nausea—straight, gut-wrenching fear. I don't know if it was fear of killing another man, fear of getting caught, fear of not killing a man that deserved to be dead, or fear of leaving Tess. I do know it was not fear of dying. I thought the worst-case scenario is I don't do it and figure out what's next.

I finally got out of bed to go to the bathroom. A steady stream of blood and urine came out. God Fucking Damnit. When the good doctor Glasgow walked me through the symptoms he mentioned bloody stools—which I've had for a while--and blood in my urine. Bloody urine means my kidneys are soon to be fucked. After the kidneys, it's a quick advance to either the liver or lungs. Then I'm done. It was clear to me this was a now or never choice, and never wasn't an option.

Shiloh picked me up at the hotel around 3 p.m. and I told him I had a few hours to kill (forgive my literal humor) before my bus took off, and that I could use a couple of hours at the cabaret. Didn't have to twist his arm. The plan nearly twisted an ugly circle as he insisted we go to the Mile High Gentlemen's Club, which was a good 20 minutes' drive. I lied and told him I'd been hooking up with a stripper named "Destiny" at the Diamond and wanted to see her.

"I know most of the girls at the Diamond and I've never met Destiny.", he said.

"You will this afternoon.", I stoically replied, "She's hotter than a lightning bolt". That was enough to cure his curiosity and keep my plan moving forward.

He told me I looked nervous and I brushed it off saying that editor meetings always make me nervous because editors are usually pricks. We pulled into the back of the parking lot and I told him I had some Don Julio 1942—one of his favorites—and we should take a quick swig before heading in. He told me to take the first shot. Fuck. I pressed my lips as hard as I could as he fucked around with his wallet and tried my best to act like I'd taken a gulp without letting that shit touch my lips. I wiped my mouth with my hand to be sure and in as raspy a voice as I could muster said, "Goddam! That shit is smooth."

He smiled a snarly grin and took my flask from my hand and took a long drink.

"Shit's got a bite.", were the last words he ever said.

I took the flask from his hand and by the time I put it up to my mouth, I turned to look at him and his nose was bleeding. Drips at first, then a run. As hard as he tried, he couldn't keep his head up. Then a thick, brownish foam started to pour out of his mouth. His hands and arms were convulsing like he had Parkinson's or something. I kept my eye on the glovebox, hoping to keep Sunshine out of his reach. He looked one last time into my eyes and his head dropped for good.

I'd just killed a man. My hands were shaking and my heart and head were pounding like a bomb was going off over and over. Fuck, I was dizzy and could barely breathe. I started dripping with sweat.

I took his keys out of the ignition and put them in my pocket. If he wasn't dead, I didn't want him to be able to drive for help. I got out, opened the back door and grabbed my pack, and took off for the bus station. About halfway there--about 5 minutes--I stopped dead in my fucking tracks. I realized I had left my satchel in the back seat of his car in my death-making daze. Fuck. Fucking Fuck.

THE LAST LETTER

I had no choice. My legs were shaking horrible like, but I walked back. I was walking toward the car and some do-gooder douchebag was tapping on his window trying to wake him up. "Mister, you okay, mister?"

Jesus, I almost started to hyperventilate. The guy started walking quickly toward the club and I knew I had to act fast. Damn fast. Goddam fast. After he turned the corner, I used Shiloh's key to unlock the doors.

I reached in the back and grabbed my satchel—the only trace I was ever there. I looked one last time at his gray face and noticed the fucker was still barely breathing. Slow, shallow breaths like long hiccups. Gasps. No fucking way. Bad guys must have nine fucking lives. I came this far and wasn't leaving until he was damn dead, and I knew I only had minutes—maybe seconds, to be sure he was very damn dead.

I looked around, grabbed my climbing strap from my pack, and, from his back seat put it around his neck and pulled hard and slow so I wouldn't leave a mark. His body jerked 3 or 4 last times and went lifeless. His face, shirt, and my strap were covered in blood from his mouth and nose.

He was dead as hell. I leaned forward and whispered, "You'll never hurt her again." Shiloh's never not gotten the last word, but I assure you that wasn't the case on his last day. I slid my strap from his lifeless throat, put it in my pack, and hiked the fuck out of there.

I made it to the Greyhound station and got on the first bus heading out. I had to wait 15 minutes for it to pull out. It was the longest 15 minutes of what's fixin' to be a very short life. I was still shaking on the bus, staring out the window ready for cop cars to surround it at any second.

I instinctively took out my flask and unscrewed the top and brought it to my lips. Caught myself. Fuck. Not only was it still filled with opiate poison, but the last person to drink from it was dead. I walked back to the bathroom of the bus and emptied it in the toilet so the evidence would now be diluted in the deep blue rinse of a Greyhound bus toilet flush. A fitting end.

The bus pulled out and headed south. I have no idea where I go from here, as long as I go as fast and as far from Denver, Colorado where my best and my worst memories will now remain.

Shiloh Gates is dead. Tess is free. I am sad about the latter and relieved by the former.

Your Murderous Friend,
Tracy

I stared at the letter in shock. I could hear my own heartbeat and could only stare out the window at the waning daylight. My mouth was dry and my skin felt cold. I was a witness to a murder. I knew every detail. Denial overcame me.

Perhaps it never happened? It was very likely he had walked away and wrote about something he wanted desperately to do but in a moment of conscience could not carry forth. I had hoped that was the case. I convinced myself that it was the case. He was a better human being than that. He was in love and had something to live for, even if he was clearly dying. The man I knew was many things, but evil was not one of them. Not once. He was not, and could not be, a murderer.

I continued on, hoping to find the absolution—the confession that he could not do it. The next parcel was a small box postmarked Tres Piedras, New Mexico. I opened it with my pocket knife and emptied the contents onto my desk. My lips started to quiver and my eyes bulged. It was a golden climbing strap covered in dry blood and a key ring with a Texas-shaped medallion and a large silver bullet on the ring, along with a dozen keys. There was simply a hastily written note that I unfolded that read, "Please get rid of this."

My friend had become a cold-blooded, calculated, premeditated murderer. He had gone to a place only hardened souls go, and he would never be able to come home to a God he had just re-acquainted with. He would never see love again. What innocence he had left was gone forever and he had to live whatever days he had left knowing that.

I was shocked. I was appalled.

I blurted out another "No. Fuck no!"

Yet, it was not enough. I could have said that word fifty times and it would not have been enough to accurately express my frustration, disappointment, and contempt for the actions of my dying friend.

The questions of my hope had been answered, and the answer was emptiness and anger toward my friend, Tracy McGuire.

While I did not—and may never—understand how in the snap of a finger my mind switched to the issue at hand. I was in possession of a murder weapon and admission of a heinous crime—evidence of a possibly unsolved mystery from several months ago in a place I had never been and now had no intent to go. My mind raced. Should I contact the authorities? Should I finally tell Debbie of the tragic end of this charade I'd been playing the past few months? Should I burn the letter and evidence as if I'd never seen it? Hell, should I burn all of the letters?

In moments like this, there is no quiet thought. No pondering. Just a mind racing in a desperate attempt to find the most reasonable solution to a vexing, immediate problem.

Ultimately, I reviewed the facts and chose the most convenient path, and did so with amazing pragmatism. I did nothing. If I told the authorities, I would have to share all of the letters--all of the evidence. I was already invited to a story I did not want to tell and this would have just prolonged it. I could not tell Debbie because I would have to share my own secret of this journey I chose to take that October day. I would have to expose my own lie by revealing his truth. More importantly, it would so jade her opinion of a friend we both held dear much of our life. Others would find out about this, and I refused to allow an otherwise good life to be remembered so notoriously due to this tragic end.

Shiloh Gates' family, and Tess Thompson, would have to find their own closure. I grabbed a shop towel and carefully placed the daisy chain and key tag back in the box so I would not leave my fingerprints on it. I did not place it back in its order in the pile; instead, placing it securely in my safe.

I lit another cigarette, my third of the day and the violation of my own rule at a time I was witness to the violation of the ultimate rule of my faith—Thou shall not kill. I am not sure I even took a drag off that last Camel. I just watched the reflection of my situation in the simmering smoke that drifted slowly across the room, diluting quietly into the air with no trace.

THE LAST LETTER

My mind was blank and my emotions had long since left. I was numb and finally, thankfully, my alarm went off. Far too much time had passed. I took one last full-circle view of my shop wondering if I had left any further evidence, and went quietly back to the house with the weight of the world on my shoulders and little else but doubt left in my mind.

CHAPTER 15

THE SHAMAN AND THE RISING SMOKE OF A FINISHED LIFE

I took a week away from the shop to clear my mind, returning resolutely to finish the last epistles of a dying man who seemed on many levels to have already perished. There were about a dozen letters left. Three were from non-descript Southwestern stops—Shiprock, New Mexico; Pagosa

THE LAST LETTER

Springs, Colorado; Mexican Hat, Utah—that included descriptions of the desolate scenery, the more desolate souls that wandered onto and off of the Greyhound bus system, and remote motels each night that offered neither comfort nor accommodation. There was no optimism. No colorful experiences and no hopeful prose, only more miles and more words to nowhere.

Based on his handwriting and details of his deteriorating condition, his end was near and I was relieved that mine would be with it. I felt guilty for wanting the journey to finally end. But I realized I no longer had the anticipation of a frivolous story, wayward antics, or a dying man's insights that had captivated me until the cold-blooded murder of Shiloh Gates. There were eight letters, all postmarked the same day as the first letter—The Last Letter—I received in my personal post office box. They were from Kayenta, Arizona in the middle of the Navajo Nation. I opened them all and sorted them in a pile by the dates he noted on each and read them from start to finish.

Larry,

I didn't expect this to be the end of my road. Hell, I'm not sure what I expected. I am sure this is the end of my road. The race to my end has finally come to this last lap.

The bus stop in Kayenta is a broken-down Phillips 66 on the dusty edge of a dreary town. It was a twenty-minute stop, so I got out to go to the bathroom, stretch my legs, and get something to drink.

I went to wash my hands and looked in the grease-smudged mirror above the stained sink of a decrepit bathroom. I didn't recognize the person I saw. Dying, killing, and a week of wandering through the desert on a bus of misfits have taken a toll. I haven't shaved since Denver. My face is deeply drawn and my eyes sunken and black. Bet I'm down to 150, far from my fightin' weight of 190. I couldn't stop staring. Who the fuck is that guy in the mirror?

I walked out to get back on the bus. An old Indian in worn jeans and tattered flannel was standing between me and the bus. He was staring right at me. His eyes were like black mirrors. His stare was intense, but weirdly calming, with not one ounce of emotion. I stared back and slowly walked toward him, as if I was drawn by a tractor beam. Hell, he looked worse than me. He had creases in his brown face you could ski down. Can't explain it, but I knew. I just fucking knew.

"It's time for us to go, isn't it?" I said.

I knew I wouldn't be riding one more mile on the bus. He gave a subtle nod and I walked into the bus, grabbed my satchel, and left my pack. Didn't seem I'd need the pack any longer. I knew this was the end or damn close, and I couldn't bear the thought of dying without hearing Tess's voice one last time and having her hear mine.

I've been tortured each night in the dim light and random sounds of cheap desert hotels, restless from both the intense pain and my guilt. The days have been worse. Blank stares out a Greyhound window for hours as the parched, sunbaked landscape and distant mountain-scapes rolled by like strips of film in a movie with no plot, rolling in slow motion with no intermission.

It wasn't until a stop in Mexican Hat that it became clear to me. My guilt wasn't from killing another man, a man who deserved to die. I still feel no remorse, neither for ending his life nor the manner in which I did it. My guilt was leaving Tess.

THE LAST LETTER

Leaving her with nothing but wonder and gaps, more questions than answers. I had shared everything with her, and she with me. I couldn't share my life with her—fate wouldn't allow it—but I could share my death. I needed to share it with her because I know it is near. Very near. The chaperone to my end is here to take me to my last waltz.

We walked across the parking lot to a beat-up old Ford F-150 that, like the old Indian, had long since seen better miles. I threw my shit in the front, looked down to see a hole in the passenger floorboard with a nice view of the cracked blacktop, and a dashboard big enough to serve a pizza on. He got in without saying a word. I leaned in with the door still opened and asked him if I had ten minutes for a phone call, just ten. He nodded and I walked to a graffiti-covered phone booth at the edge of the parking lot and closed the door.

I put as much change in the phone as I could—probably three or four bucks—and called Marg's and asked for the manager. After a pause that lasted a lifetime, she picked up. Her voice was warm and sad like every vocal cord was straining just to say "hello". I almost hung up. I felt my chest clench, then the tightness moved from my chest to my throat, then to my jaws.

I had wanted her voice to be the last thing I heard before I died, but I couldn't speak. It was like the first time I saw her at the table in Marg's, but this time it wasn't a third-grade crush. It was wanting to say a thousand words at once and not being able to speak even one. All I could muster was a whisper, "Tess, it's me." She started sobbing on the phone.

She paused and said, "Where are you. I want to see you. I need to be with you."

I had no more lies to tell. I told her the truth. I was at a bus stop in Kayenta in the Navajo Nation. I was going with an old Indian to die, and that she wouldn't understand because I don't. She asked me to hold on as long as I could, and that she would find a way to be there with me. I reminded her that isn't how all this works.

There was a pause. "Was it you that killed him?"

All I could say was, "We all have to die, some just deserve it more than others."

"You won't die alone, Tracy. I will be the last thing you see when you close your eyes, and my heart will beat with yours until it stops. You are the only man I have loved, and I have loved every kiss, every laugh, and every breath we have taken together. You were right—forever is never long enough."

"I love you, Tess Thompson. You will be the last, and best, breath I take."

I slowly hung up. The fist in my chest was gone, the iron grip clenched against my throat…gone. Her voice alive in my heart, I opened the door to the booth and took two steps out.

And stopped.

Because I knew.

I stared at the dusty lot and took a deep breath in, and exhaled slowly.

It was time. Time to die.

With Tess's voice the last sound in my ears, my heart full, I was finally ready for what comes next. I walked to the truck, stared at the Indian and off we went.

About ten minutes into the drive, my past escaped and my focus was again on the moment. It was time to learn more about my new friend and the road ahead.

"What's your name, my new Native American friend?

Nothing.

"I'm Tracy. Tracy S. McGuire. And, today that "S" is for

'suspicious', because I have a weird feeling on this one. You feeling it, too?"

Nothing.

"Where are we going?"

Again…nothing.

"Any idea why we're going to where you're not telling me we're going?"

The old grizzled face and impossibly deep, wise eyes turned to me. He looked at me…just looked. And--again—I just fucking knew. Questions that didn't need answers. Questions that didn't HAVE answers. No answers that mattered. My path was clear, and we both knew it.

After forty minutes of silence driving down the dirt roads of the Nation, I couldn't take the silence anymore.

"Well, if you don't have a name," I told him, "then I got you covered. You are Ben. Your name will be Ben. Like been-there, done-that, because this doesn't look like your first Last Roundup rodeo."

Nothing.

Ben there. Done that.

"Or, Ben-Jammin', like 'We Be Jammin'. You ever heard any Bob Marley?"

Not a damn thing.

"Are you supposed to talk, or am I? Cuz I'll talk like a mother fucker if you don't."

No grin, no eyebrow raise. Nothing. Ben's not big on personality. But Ben's taking me somewhere to die. I know it as clearly as I've ever known anything.

"You going to kill me, or just let me die? Cuz, if you're going to kill me, I have a few good ideas for you. Just killed a guy myself a while back."

Nothing.

We got to a metal and adobe, well, maybe someone would call it a house—two rooms, no shitter and a well out back. Sits at the base of a pale red mesa. About 30 yards from the place is a rickety-framed dome hut. Ben pointed me to a wood-framed bed with a raspy ass mattress and went in to start the wood-burning stove.

Not as good as dying in a whorehouse, but not as bad as dying in a jail cell. It is what it is.

Just Me,
Tracy

The next few letters detailed his last days with the Indian he had named Ben and his worsening condition. It was a ritualistic end with medicinal teas and what he described simply as "grains" in the morning. He would write during the afternoons under the hot autumn desert sun and spent his evenings on a blanket in the sweat hut—the dome-shaped structure near Ben's shack.

He described sweating in the heat of a small fire in the hut while Ben chanted and placed a mud concoction on his torso and cheeks. Each evening included a hallucinogenic drink I assume was peyote-based and, eventually, a strained walk back to the cot in the shack. Near the end, there was a letter that detailed a vivid hallucination of his death.

Larry,

I was able to die last night, in my awakened dreams, and if that is why I am here and how I will die, I am at peace with it.

I drifted in and out after drinking a half a bowl of Ben's brew and each time I opened my eyes I saw sparks from the

THE LAST LETTER

fire swirling around me while my Indian friend chanted. The sparks weren't random. They were flying in formation. Different shapes that would come and go as the embers glowed and went through the top of the hut. Some were scary—snakes, wolves, ravens. Fangs, teeth, and claws that struck so close to my face I'd close my eyes and jerk back. So fucking real. Others followed each time—eagles, elk, bears, and more. Each time they'd attack the other and the sparks would stop for a minute and the whole thing would play out again. I yelled at Ben to explain, but he only stops chanting in the hut long enough to cover me in red paste and put more kindling on the fire.

Then, there were no sparks. It was full daylight. There was no hut, no fire, and no chanting. I was naked on the edge of a sandstone bluff on a bed of old, dead branches. The sun was blinding. The only sound was a hawk. It was piercing, but I couldn't tell if it was over me or next to me. Nothing but the blinding light of the sun and the sharp, loud shrieks of a hawk.

Smoke started to rise from my body. Slowly at first, then plumes of steel gray smoke. I realized the branches beneath me were on fire, but I wasn't. There were flames, but there was no heat. There was no pain. I wasn't burning to death. I wasn't choking. My breath was slow and deep as the smoke got heavier and moved higher. I was calm. Transcendent. I tried to look down from the air through the smoke, but couldn't see anything. The smoke felt cool. None of it made sense, but at the time it all made sense. I was there. And it was just as real as this moment, laying on the cot with a slight sliver of morning sun warming my face through the panes of the window.

The pain is intense and constant, Larry. The meds barely touch it. I can feel the strangling grip of the cancer on every organ, bone, and muscle in my body. Ben's concoctions help a little, but the only time the pain seems to fade is in the sweat and visions in the hut. Don't understand that.

I think death, like life, comes with pain. Can't avoid it. It's the price you have to pay for the hope of peace, and we all have to pay it. I will find my peace. I'm sure of it. I've seen it. I want it. It's now so close I feel like I can touch it.

Tracy

The penultimate letter was brief and barely legible. The writing was strained as if it took hours to complete.

Larry,

On the bus, I decided I had one last chance for atonement so I wrote a letter to apologize to some of the people that I know I've hurt. I was able to address some, and others I just put in the envelope to be addressed later. I went way back for several, and as recent as the week I left Chicago for a few others.

Yesterday, we went to the hut in the afternoon. Ben had to help me walk to get there. It was light so I was going to write. The fire had barely started and I showed Ben the contents of my satchel and made him promise to send the letters once I was gone. I told him the most important letter was the first letter I wrote to you. The only letter in a light blue envelope. The only letter I hope you get. Already stamped. No fucking excuses, Ben!

He reached into the satchel and took all the letters. He took the letters I've written from here and put them back in the satchel with that first letter to you. He kept the other letters in his hand, the letters I wrote on the bus those many days ago. He dropped them slowly in the fire. I was fucking pissed, but didn't have the strength to do anything about it.

He looked at me and said his first and only words.

THE LAST LETTER

"They already forgave you." followed by, "And my name isn't Ben."

Then his stoic, cragged face finally found a smile and he put his callused hand on my forehead. He reached into my satchel and took my flask out.

I grinned a half-assed grin and said, "Careful. The last guy that took a swig out of that died."

He put the flask in the fire. I hope my regrets and apologies find their way to where they need to be.

I don't know how many letters I have left in me, so if you can find your way to it, tell—

Tell Glasgow it was worth it. Option B WAS the better option.

Tell Jeannie I appreciate it. And, Franey, too.

Tell your kids there are no second chances. Treat every chance like it's your first chance and your only chance. Regrets only turn into baggage when you carry them with you.

Tell my dad this isn't "just it". I'm coming back, and we all do.

Tell my mom I forgave her long ago. A mother and child will always be bound more by love than blood.

Tell God I'm sorry. I had no business blaming him.

And tell God Thank You. It was all so damn good. Every. Fucking. Day. Even the bad ones.

Tell Tess she was the one. My person. We will meet again under better circumstances. I miss her more than she can know. Forever is never long enough.

Tell Debbie you love her. Often. And never stop.

Tell yourself life is short. Drink every drop. Play through the pain. Leave nothing on the field.

Tell Grandma Bea I'm looking forward to seeing her again. And that I was right—I did miss her every damn day.

Tell anyone that will listen—Always steer clear of anyone named Butch in a bar.

Your Friend. Your Co-Pilot. Sorry I dragged you into all of this, but glad you were there for me. You made a difference. The difference.

Tracy

It was in my hands. This was it.

The Last Letter.

The end of the journey. No, the end of A journey. There are more journeys ahead, for me, for Tess Thompson. Even, I am now convinced, for Tracy. In some form. In some fashion.

The Last Letter.

My heart was pounding as Tracy's must have been when he was waiting for the bastard Shiloh Gates to take that last, fatal, criminal swig from a poisoned flask.

All these months, reading my friend's journey of discovery, of rebirth, of life, of death. All these months traveling both within and without. I was there with him. I was in the stands, a spectator to the brutal battle of life and death and love of my friend in the arena.

The Last Letter.

In the sweaty clasp of my fingers.

And a final surprise.

The Last Letter was NOT from my friend.

The final letter from the Nation was different. The handwriting of the address was different, feminine. I had wondered if it may have been Ben's writing but knew it couldn't have been. It was a thick envelope with several pages and I knew from Tracy's description that his Indian friend wouldn't write this much, and from the previous letter, I doubted Tracy had the strength to fill an envelope with text.

Larry,

I am writing to tell you that your friend Tracy has passed away. It was a peaceful death. I was able to take his last breath with him, and his heart beat with mine until it stopped. My hand was on his heart, and his hand was on mine, letting our souls speak one last time before his eyes finally closed.

I received a call from Tracy several days ago. He sounded frail and strained. He was afraid, and I wasn't going to let him die without me by his side. I told my family and they agreed to watch my children as long as it took for me to find him so I could be with him. I had to see him and touch him one last time.

My family adored Tracy. They adored him because they knew what I have known since the day I met him—I loved Tracy McGuire as much as any man has been loved by a woman. I think it is important for you to know that your friend died deeply loved.

He spoke of you often. He said that you were a writer like him, but better. Tracy was filled with curiosity and awe. We would often take trips into the mountains and his joy and awe were amazing to me. I felt like he was letting me see the world through his eyes. I saw the world with him. Through him.

He would often say that he wished you could see what we saw because you could describe it so much better than he could.

Please take no offense, but I can't imagine that. Tracy was an incredible storyteller. He loved to talk. My God, he could talk. No man has ever shared so much wonder with me. I will remember every story he told me, and he told me thousands. The names are still a jumble, but your name came up frequently. He had great respect for you, and he loved your family.

I have been married twice and courted by countless men. They have all been attracted by my appearance. They have all wanted to love what I was, never who I was. I had given up hope that I would ever be loved by a man as anything more than a trophy. Until Tracy. Tracy was different. He didn't want my body and never felt like it was his to take.

Tracy loved me for who I am, and he let me love him with no conditions and no ownership. He found beauty in me where other men had never bothered to look. I had given up looking for my inner beauty, and my experiences with every man in my life made me question if I even had it. He found my beauty and expressed it to me in ways that made it real to me. Your friend was like no man I have ever met. He was beautiful.

I had stopped looking for love long ago. It was when I stopped looking into the night sky that my star had finally come. It was a blinding star and I knew that such light would eventually explode into a dimming glow that would fade and draw into the darkness of night. I knew that I loved him from the moment I saw him. He was like an angel, sent from God to prove to me that true, deep love exists. That it is incredible. He was, and is, the only star in my night sky. Surrounded by the deep hue of darkness, I know that light will continue to glow and provide me with warmth in the days and years ahead.

It took everything I could do to find him. Fortunately, a man at the gas station in Kayenta remembered Tracy and

THE LAST LETTER

drew a map for me to find Sani's house. Tracy kept calling him Ben, which didn't seem to annoy Sani like it might have for you and for me. Sani is a kind and quiet man. He trusts me. He allowed me to help him take Tracy to wherever he is to go next. It has been a solemn privilege to be here. It has meant everything to me.

Tracy was barely lucid by the time I finally made it here. When he was coherent, he asked me to write to you to let you know when he had passed. He said you would need closure. He said to tell you he was sorry. Tracy lived with few regrets and I know horrible things he has done, so I hope you will accept his apology. He passed three days after I arrived.

After Tracy passed, Sani and I drove his body to the top of a nearby mesa. It was the most remote place I have ever been. Sani laid Tracy's body on a large stack of dried branches. I prayed. Tracy used to kiss me on the forehead, then the cheek, then the end of my nose. He called it the "holy trinity of love", and I always felt like I was being blessed.

I leaned onto the wood stack and kissed his forehead, then his cheek, then a final soft kiss on his lips. I will never love a man again like I loved Tracy McGuire.

Sani had soaked Tracy's shirt in kerosene and gave it to me with a match. I lit the shirt and threw it on the branches. The fire lit quickly and the heat was intense. The heat radiated within me, then through me. It was Tracy giving my heart one last, warm embrace. It was amazing. At that moment, Tracy was with me. He was me. We were one.

It is time for me to go home now. My devastation, my loss, is only beginning. I will need the embrace of my children and my hope that I will one day see him again in another life to go on. Our memories together are indelible. They bring me joy and comfort. I know that I can't live in the past and that someday I will have to leave it, but not today.

It is the memories we will never create together that have broken my heart. He will not be there to fish for trout on the Blue River again with my dad or tell my mom every detailed ingredient of each of his grandma Bea's recipes after dinner. He was teaching both my children how to throw a perfect spiral with a football, and I know he had many lessons of greater value to share with them. He will never look into my eyes again to assure me with his gaze that he saw my beauty. He made me feel as if I was the only woman on earth. When we took our last breath together, those future memories drifted into the desert sky, rising with the smoke of the fire.

When someone so special gives you so much in such a short time you don't take time to think about how much more they would have been able to give until they're gone. It is the emptiness of my future, not the beautiful memories of my time with Tracy, that have embedded such sorrow in my soul. I fear the joy and sorrow will forever fight for my heart, and my hope is that eventually joy—my memories of Tracy--will win.

Tracy left his motorcycle to me when he left Denver. I have kept it in my garage. Late each night, I have gone to the garage to sit on his—and now my--motorcycle. It's like Tracy—it has scars and dents, and chrome and power, and comfort. When I sit on it and close my eyes, it feels like I am with him. It feels like I am home. I can see the beautiful vistas and feel his joy. His wonder. His warmth. My memories are the last glow of his light, and I will never let that light fade.

I loved your friend, Tracy McGuire, and have to continue to live knowing I will never love like that again. I know that he will always be alive in my heart. He used to tell me, "Forever is never long enough." He was right. And he was loved. God, I do miss him so.

*Love,
Tess Thompson*

CHAPTER 16

THE JOURNEY'S END AND THE PATH FORWARD

Tess's letter had provided me with unexpected comfort. I read her words, written in perfectly aligned cursive, and could feel her suffering. It was as though she was willing

THE LAST LETTER

the pain upon herself. Perhaps Tracy was right. Through pain--through suffering--we find our path to our truths, and acknowledging the voice of those truths is ultimately what liberates us.

I had finally reached the end of the letters and the life and, therefore, death of Tracy McGuire. I waited several minutes for a pause of reflection, a tear, or some sign of my closure. I felt very little sense of mourning, perhaps because I had already mourned the passing of his spirit that day in Yosemite and the death of his soul when he took another man's life.

I felt thankful to have learned more about a friend I previously felt I knew very well. We all thought we knew him very well because he was so quick to share every story and every event in embellished detail. However, it was the stories he did not tell that ultimately created who he was—a person none of us, in fact, really knew. We all have stories we refuse to tell that are then left to haunt and define us in ways we often do not realize or understand.

What feeling of loss I did experience was garnered from gaining a greater sense, not just of who my friend was, but why. He found his peace not in dying, as we all must do, but in becoming more human.

His greatest and most fearful adventure wasn't on a mountain or a motorcycle, it was the discovery of what lay within him. It was a journey he chose to avoid until he was introduced to his own end.

His last several months had stripped him bare. Naked and vulnerable, his soul was able to reveal his truth. His truth was both darkness and light, love and hate, fear and joy. He had finally accepted who he was, both in his pure beauty and his many blemishes.

It was in his truth that he found peace, which is perhaps the greatest testament to a life well-lived.

By inviting me into his menagerie of demise, he also helped me live. He helped me better appreciate my life--what I have, who I am, and who I would like to be. I will write more stories, but now they will be my stories to tell and I will write them in my own words.

He forced me to awaken a passion I thought I had lost, and I will be forever grateful to him for helping me reclaim that fire within. It was a journey worth taking, while reluctant at first, to help me see my own path forward and to better understand my truths.

I will not need Camels and the dark winter nights in my shop to continue to write. Life is too short to keep secrets. Smoking was a dalliance that served its purpose for this very unique and challenging assignment, but that service will no longer be necessary for the path I have chosen. I will not have an obligation to write on behalf of a dying friend. I can simply savor the joy of doing something I love.

By going through his struggle toward death for the past few months, I unknowingly found a deeper purpose for my own life, a life that—prior to opening that last letter—had been very comfortable and satisfying. I now hug my kids more often each day, and a little harder and a little longer than I had before. And, I have nurtured a deeper, greater love for Debbie than I had thought was possible.

While I felt relieved, I realized there were still decisions that had to be made and work to be done before I could conclude. Death is always hardest on the living who have the difficult tasks to work through in order to transition from the harsh reality of loss to the fondness created by a lifetime of memories; to heal and find comfort.

I have secured his letters, and his evidence, to let his past rest in peace, allowing only the fond memories of those that held him dear to remain. I went to the bank to see what, if anything, was left of his balance. There was over twenty-five thousand dollars. I put it toward a worthy cause—anonymously, as he would want it. John Franey and I created a scholarship at the local high school for students pursuing a career in literature. I still have the map hanging in my shop, but I have removed the pictures and left the pins. His journey will stay to help remind me of mine.

And I have done all of this thankful for a very extraordinary, ordinary day in early October and the first—and last—letter from a dear friend that lived and that died on his own terms and in his own words.

The End

ACKNOWLEDGEMENTS

In appreciation of my unofficial editing team, whose insights provided depth and detail to this unique story:

Kristen G.
Michele B.
Dale M.
Lisa P.
Karen J.
Gary H.
Rhonda D.
Rachel M.
Hammer
Nick M.
Rick G.
Jill M.

Thank you all, and thank you for reading this story that had taken far too long to be told.

Printed in Great Britain
by Amazon